I0650364

Harry B. Magill

Biography of Francis Schlatter the Healer

With his life, works and wanderings

Harry B. Magill

Biography of Francis Schlatter the Healer
With his life, works and wanderings

ISBN/EAN: 9783337194376

Printed in Europe, USA, Canada, Australia, Japan

Cover: Foto ©Raphael Reischuk / pixelio.de

More available books at **www.hansebooks.com**

PRICE 50 CENTS.

FRANCIS SCHLATTER

THE HEALER.

PUBLISHED BY
SCHLATTER PUBLISHING CO.,
DENVER, COLO.

BIOGRAPHY

OF

FRANCIS SCHLATTER,

THE HEALER,

WITH HIS

LIFE, WORKS AND WANDERINGS.

PUBLISHED BY
SCHLATTER PUBLISHING CO.,
DENVER, COLO.
1896.

THE MERCHANTS PUB. CO., PRINTERS.
DENVER, COLORADO.
1896.

PREFACE.

In presenting this biography to the public of the life, works and wanderings of Francis Schlatter, "The Healer" (or, as the newspapers and journals styled him, "The New Mexican Messiah, or The Christ Man"), together with a brief sketch of his early life prior to the time when he entered upon his mission to heal the sick, to open the eyes of the blind and to comfort those who were sorely afflicted, I wish to call the attention of my readers to the earnestness and simplicity of manner in which he performed his work while in Denver, and other cities as well. The many trials with which Francis had to contend with, not only in the eyes of man, but with himself, shows how a person who is inclined to do good and what is right can master the physical and live in the inner world. This is an object lesson to humanity, which, if practiced and lived up to, there would be less sickness and misery in the world to-day, and all would be sunshine and gladness. In compiling this work the author is greatly indebted to Mr. Fox for all the main facts, illustrations, etc., and for local matter I have had to rely largely upon the "Rocky Mountain News."

The most noted pulpit orator west of the Mississippi river delivered a sermon which was full of sympathy and loving kindness in behalf of the work in which the Healer was engaged, and said: "He has helped me morally." The depth of meaning contained within that sentence can never be expressed in words, nor ever be manifested upon the surface, but only to be enjoyed in the kingdom of heaven within. To this end this work is earnestly dedicated, with the Faith that it will be the means of a blessing to humanity.

THE AUTHOR.

INTRODUCTORY NOTE.

About a year ago the public was startled by the appearance of a man who created no little excitement, which in time was followed by intense interest and belief. This peculiar man (in plainness of attire only) was the subject of discussion from the Atlantic ocean to the Pacific, and from the great lakes to the Gulf of Mexico. People from all parts of the country flocked to see this wonderful Healer, and to return home a living testimony as to his powers and methods of healing.

It is one of the many facts that presents the social environments of the times and, to a great extent, illuminates the aspirations and the impulses contained within the human breast.

It is also a fact which reproves the self-civility of institutional religion of the day, the fortified creeds of science.

This, of course, can only be seen by those of broad views, and not by those of narrow minds.

The ignorant will wonder and marvel; the shallow will cavil, wrangle, or mock and grin;

and the wise only will carry the facts deep down into their hearts and souls, and meditate on their wide and pathetic import, as there is a majestic and lofty warmth in this Denver scene, and the pathos attached to the event will long be remembered with the scenes that disclose or reveal the tenderness of the human heart in its original and sincere artlessness; such a high and dramatic feeling as has been made known to gentle souls in the short but lightened and shining command, "Suffer little children to come unto me."

Each day witnessed an anxious and surging crowd, numbering from 2,000 to 5,000 people, of all creeds and colors, who were bent on seeing this artless, ardent and zealous man, who, by giving up himself entirely to the interests of the Holy Spirit, has attained an extraordinary power to heal the sick, to restore the eyesight of the blind, make the deaf to hear, giving speech to the dumb, pliableness to the palsied.

The people did not come because they believed him to be Christ, but because, agreeable to reason, the remembrance of Christ has left a foundation for belief in such works.

The purity of his manners, the freeness from guile, the outward and complete surrender to the Father, suggest a ready deference, a deep respect and a profound, merciful love.

It is utterly impossible for any but a mind exasperated by opinion or superstition, or vitiated by contempt of just restraint, to doubt or to interrogate the purity and unselfishness of his spirit. To doubt the condition of his mental faculties is another question.

But it is momentous to emphasize that, bolting the claim that he is the Saviour reincarnated, his being present forces upon me—and I may say upon all who saw him—the idea or influence of an extremely but completely sound mind. As, however, his personality is deserving of the most cautious notice, and worthy of all scientific observation, I should say that he has one more manner of what, strictly observed, we should have to mark out or show as an illusion or error in our present assured beliefs of the psycho-mental offices.

In describing the institution or schooling he went through for this ecclesiastical function of healing, he invariably said, I "had to" do this and I "had to" do that. Prudent information, however, discloses that this "had to" was not, accurately speaking, an order or command from objective "voices," such as guided Joan of Arc, but simply an influence or impression of the will of the Father, which is subjective.

Of course, this will be immediately acknowledged as only a weakly, enlarged effect of a religious appearance, common to those who endeavor or essay to yield or deliver up the personal will to any eager extent to the direction of the Father, as eminent from those who attempt to control their behavior by reason of principle altogether.

Not all cases handled were restored to health, or even noticeably eased. Some were cured immediately, and some were alleviated almost immediately.

The cure was frequently by degrees, "as the Faith came." When helped or cured, sufferers, to express their gratitude, thanked him (as he *never* accepted money). The Healer replied: "Don't thank me; thank the heavenly Father. Put your faith in Him, not in me. I have no power but what He gives me through my Faith. He will give you the same."

There was no trick to gain applause, no insincerity of secret, no exertion for public exposure in the Healer's behavior.

A passageway was built, so that only one person at a time could approach the Healer. Francis stood at the end of the passage-way (in front of the residence), in full view of the people, took each one that passed through, and, without asking any questions, took the individual's hands in his own hands (which were crossed) for a long or a short time, invariably closing his eyes or raising them upward, and in a low tone uttered a brief, silent petition for Divine grace.

He stood there hatless and coatless, on an average of six hours every day, treating the afflicted. Day after day found many of the same people standing in line for hours e'er they reached the Healer.

Before the break of day there was a large crowd in front of Mr. Fox's residence in North Denver, where Schlatter was a guest during his mission in this city. While with Mr. Fox, the Healer cured the gentleman of deafness entirely.

Before sending the crowd away each day, the Healer went among the vehicles and treated the sick and afflicted who were unable to stand for hours in line and await their turn.

The manner of the Healer was quiet, peaceful and full of fellow-feeling, and affected no singularity whatever beyond that his hair was very long and fell in long curls upon his shoulders.

This appearance gives to his face, in repose or rest, an impressive similarity to the pictures of the Christ of eighteen hundred years ago. In all probability this affected the conception of those who had the privilege of visiting him. The numbers that stood around all day—never less than between 1,200 to 1,500 at one time—were earnest, even those who were curious were eagerly curious and as respectful as at a church congregation. Such was a devout, beautiful and lasting exhibition to which the noble splendors of the vast Rocky Mountain region, apparent in the near distance, formed a suitable background.

There was grandeur in the whole result, overflowing with holy and sacred feeling. The scene formed lasting mental images and pictures with many. It moved and roused the fountains in the souls of all liberal and open-hearted beings and ingenuous creatures as well. Many wept tears of joy, some of sadness, but the latter were, indeed, few.

Fathers and mothers came with lame children in their arms, some with languishing babes upon the breast; the feeling crowd parted from right to left to allow a place in line. To the observant eye the flush of doubt was upon many, and they came toward the Healer, the throat growing larger with choking excitement of the mind, the tears subdued in solicitous eyes—ah, if this might be the Savior of the manger who said: "Suffer little children to come unto me."

Schlatter was but a poor, plain, unselfish brother, who obtained a little and unfinished portion of the God-power by delivering himself entirely to the Father's will. According to the church of to-day, the forty-day fast of the Savior in the wilderness is still among the miracles. Such as it is, Schlatter has undergone in the plainest and most modest way, as with effect and under more trials than those which surrounded the Savior.

There was lots of room for doubt regarding the fast on both sides, if the external power of existing were now a liberal inquiry, which it is not.

What is worthy of particular notice in Schlatter's fast was that he remained at his mission post of healing during the entire fast. At first he would take a walk or ride from village to village along the Rio Grande in New Mexico and while in this state. In the town of Albuquerque he stopped at the house of Mr. J. A. Summers, who was then deputy clerk of the Probate Court, a family of good understanding and high in rank of esteem.

The last day of the fast was a scene not expressive, and the last moments were filled with merciful concern to those who were allowed to continue with him. Danger was perceived in his eating a solid meal.

"Have no fear," he said, "have Faith. The Father has sustained me through forty days and this is his will."

Schlatter sat down at the table alone, which was beautifully decorated with flowers brought by his friends and spread on the spotless, white table cloth. His meal was a solid one. It was served at 5 o'clock in the afternoon. Schlatter partook very heartily of fried chicken, beefsteak and eggs, together with a bottle of wine. Before withdrawing for the evening he was served with bread and milk and suffered no inconvenience.

If the abstinence from food was real—the genuineness of which is not questioned—the digestion of that supper was the nearest approach to an act beyond the understood laws of nature of anything I have ever been acquainted with. It points out clearly that what we term a purely external suggestion may have at times a larger, if not unmeasurable kindred with the spiritual.

The Healer never cared for notoriety, it was forced upon him; never doing anything in an exciting manner, but pure and meek in all things; never promulgating from the roofs of houses, but when questioned, the Healer, with a quiet and firm voice, says: "I am."

CHAPTER I.

Francis Schlatter, the Divine Healer, was
born in Alsace, France (now a province of
Germany), in the canton of Schlestadt, at
Ebersheim, April 29, 1856. His parents were
poor people who tilled the soil, spun and wove
coarse fabrics. His parents are dead, although he has one brother, a nephew and two
sisters living in Alsace. Francis never attended school after his fourteenth year. While
in his teens he learned the trade of shoe-mak-
ing. He never married; arrived in America
in 1891 and settled at Jamestown, Long Island, a small fishing place, the chief occupa-
tion of whose inhabitants is to ensnare the fes-
tive scallop. Here his townsmen always
spoke of his as "Frank," a rather good fellow, who made very good shoes, and inciden-
tally, quite a lot of money at his trade of shoemaker. The Healer remained in this fishing
hamlet on the Peconic bay about the space of
three years. Being of a decided Franco-Ger-
man accent, it was naturally very hard for

him at first to get along, but gradually with
his broken English he managed to get a start.
He was then a tall, robust fellow, and impressed every one with his sobriety and good
nature. "Aunt Sally Corwin" rented the upper half of her two-story frame house on the
main road, leading from the station to the
bay, and it was in this humble spot that the
Healer put out his sign and kept house for
himself. It was at this point that he became
acquainted with a family by the name of
Ryan, through their elder son, William, who
was an engineer on a fishing steamer which
ran for the menhaden fisheries from Green-
port. As Mr. Ryan was chief fireman on the
Annie Wilcox and afterwards the Cora P.
White (which belonged to the Church Brothers), he was in position to give employment to
Francis as fireman on the fishing steamer,
which from all reports Schlatter seemed to
enjoy for two seasons, but as time went on he
finally tired of the fireman's life and it was
then that he started at his trade of shoe-
making, which, he said, was learned in a town
near his native village. A certain Dr. Law-
ton, of New York, every few days brought cus-
tom made shoes for Francis to sew in "Aunt
2

Sally's" upper parlors, for which he was usually paid $2.50 per pair, and on the average the earnings amounted to $15 a week. His expenses were very small, the money accumulated very rapidly, but after a time living alone and bachelor housekeeping palled on the Healer, he finally thought he would like to board with the Ryans. In the Ryan family were four young ladies. Though not particularly interested in any of them, he managed to entertain them all by playing at the game of croquet, of which he was passionately fond.

A short time thereafter he started for Denver, Colorado, and stayed till the following July, when he "had to" go forth on his mission of self-denial and healing the sick; began to consider the Christ life first in Denver, but realized later that the Father had guided him especially for the preceding five years, but at that time not aware of His guidance. The Healer was born and raised a Catholic and is a Catholic still. When a baby of one year of age he was blind and deaf and was cured by the Faith of his mother, who in answer to her prayers for his cure, consecrated the child to God.

CHAPTER II.

It was in the month of July, 1893, that Schlatter disappeared, by way of Eighteenth avenue, in Denver, for parts unknown. The rain fell in torrents, and with about $3 in money, nothing certain in his future, but with a steadfast belief in his own destiny and in the promise conveyed to him by occult and unseen forces, that he would be cared for, he tramped in this condition for many days.

The elect waited to hear from him as the performer of some great miracles or wonders of the mysterious science. The scoffers have expected to hear of his incarceration in some asylum, or the recovery of his body somewhere upon the great plains, where he may have wandered in a fit of mental incapacity. None who knew him were surprised when the manner of his reappearance among the living was made known by a reporter. To those who had labored and studied with him in Denver, it seemed like the fulfillment of the promises of the still small voice that he had often said had separated him from ordinary mortals and told him to be patient; that the day would come for him to heal and reveal. The friends he had made outside of his religious societies were re- lieved to know that he yet lived and was ap- parently not suffering for the material things of life.

On one occasion the Healer, prior to this de- parture from Denver, disappeared and walked to Cheyenne, Wyoming, and back. He had not told any of his friends in this city of the pro- posed journey, and there was quite a time over it. When they were looking for him he walked in, and stated that he had walked up to Chey- enne and back. It is more than likely that he was merely toughening his feet for the longer journey he anticipated, and on which he started that rainy day over three years ago.

Francis told a thrilling story of his wander- ings, fasts, temptations and visions while be- ing tried by heavenly fire in the wilderness of the great Southwest. He said his power in- creased each day, and his Father showed him by revelation, miracles which will resound throughout the length and breadth of every land, and among all tongues. In the barren wastes of the Mojave and Yuma deserts he

wrestled with Eblis, the evil one, and over-
threw his dominion, through the mercy of God.
It was a triumph which, he claimed, would
bring a great peace to the sons of men.

Can it be that the strange Healer is the fore-
runner of the millennium, during which time
Satan is to be chained and universal peace
reign, preparatory to the end of this earthly
kingdom and rule? These signs of the times,
just as deep now as at any other time, if the
teachings of Holy Writ are followed, will be
left to those who read the strange sayings of
the man.

While Francis worked at his trade in this
city he had many spiritual communications,
yet vague, although positive enough to induce
him to swing Indian clubs and dumbbells for
two hours every day, after which the same
power impelled him to walk five to ten miles,
when the hardships of training led him to an
early rest. The Healer said: "I did not know
why I did this thing, but I know now. I was
not very strong, and Father was preparing me
for what was to come. But I had the power
to heal before I left Denver. One day Father
told me to sell out my business and not to take
anything with me, but to go, and I started."

Francis never begged during the two years of
his wanderings, and, after getting fully upon
his way, avoided the large cities and towns, because the healing power had not manifested itself in full confidence. He felt that he was not
prepared by the Father. His route was east-
ward from Denver, through the center of Kansas, touching at Clay Center, Topeka, Law-
rence and Kansas City. During this portion of
his journey, and all of the time afterward, he
asked for no food. It was given him volunta-
rily. He remained in Kansas City but a few
hours. From that point he took a southerly direction, passing through Paola, Fort Scott, and
entered the Indian Territory almost south of
the last named city. Nothing eventful disturbed the Healer until Tahlequah was
reached. Here Francis was taken very ill, by
reason of the exposure, irregularity of meals,
and the failure of power to move one leg. At
this point he was prostrated for two days, but
healed several of the Indians, who treated him
with respect and kindness. "The night of the
second day," said Schlatter, "I saw a vision, in
which I was told to start in the morning." He
arose refreshed and with no symptoms of de-
bility, bade his Indian friends farewell and

pursued his southern course. "Something made me go in that direction," he explained, and it seemed that this inclination was so pronounced that he soon found himself walking on the mountains into Hot Springs, Arkansas, in his bare head and bare feet, begrimed with travel stains, and he presented the appearance of a demented person.

"I suppose I looked tough," said Francis, "without shoes and hat. It was at this point my troubles commenced. I had trouble after trouble. The sheriff arrested me because, he said, I was insane. I was in prison there for five months and a half and was never brought before any judge." The truth was that the friendless wanderer was tried by a kangaroo court and given fifty lashes because he had no money to pay the fine of that mock institution. His good nature won for him the confidence usually reposed in the privileged prisoners called "trusties." Here Francis was made to saw wood, wash dishes and clean the deputy sheriff's house from garret to cellar. "O, I worked hard. Father told me to work hard, and I did. But I knew I would get out before long, for Father told me." The travesty upon the justice of Arkansas was exposed, probably

unwittingly, by the prisoner. Francis was im-
mured for five months and a half without a
hearing of any sort. His gullible nature, if
one would have it so, was played upon to ex-
cess by those officers of the law, who beheld in
this man an unlearned, friendless and forsaken
tramp; but after he was removed from the
confining penalties of the prison to their own
homes, he, the prisoner of the state and a vag-
abond of creation, was used as a private slave.
He became the scullion of the deputy sheriff,
who, it is presumed, saved his family a good
deal of housework and an extra outlay of
servant hire. The docile prisoner was a neat,
industrious worker, for he said so himself and
his Denver acquaintances certainly give him
that much credit, after the evidences of so
much industry here.

So the deputy sheriff virtually resurrected
slavery and trifled with the law, but the erring
servant of public opinion could not conceal his
debt five months longer. "I overheard him say
to the sheriff one day, 'Hadn't we better let him
go?' Francis laughed then, for Father had
told me already that I would soon be free. The
night before I found out I was to go, and that
is the funniest part of it all, I had a dream, and

in the dream I saw a canary bird flying loosely in a room, and from that room it flew through an open door to another, and from there through another door into still another room. Some persons were trying to catch the bird, but it got through an open window and escaped. I knew Father had sent me the dream to tell me that I was the canary bird, and that I would soon be free; so when I heard the deputy sheriff speaking to the sheriff about letting me go, I told them of the dream, saying that the Father would free me, no matter what they might do to prevent it. Just after this the sheriff asked me if I did not want to go into some little business in Hot Springs." The Healer said that he had already given up one business and given everything away with it. "'Why should I desire to go into business again?' I asked. He offered to set me up in something, but I said no. Father told me what to say. One day I was taken over to the deputy sheriff's house. They had begun to watch me now. Well, we were in the same room, the deputy and I, when his wife called him: 'John! John!' she said; 'come in here and watch Jean for a few moments.' He forgot me, and suddenly Father said: 'Now start!' And I went out of the door and walked very fast. I did not run," laughed Francis, "but I did walk very fast, for I was glad to be free. But I was not entirely free yet, so I kept on up the mountain side, walking at the same gait until I reached the top, where I laid down for only a few moments. Then I started down the other side, halting half way towards the foot in a little gully. I got behind the trunk of a fallen tree and slept until 11 o'clock the following day. That day I wandered, and all of that night, getting food at negro cabins, and then going back into the hills. I treated some of these people, because of their kindness to me. The second day I was twenty miles from Hot Springs, near the Sulphur Springs. Then I suddenly commenced going north. I was surprised, because Father had always told me to go south. I asked Him why He made me go in that direction, when before it had always been the other way, but He told me to go on; it was not for me to quarrel with the Father, so I obeyed. And then Satan, how he came to me now, when I was troubled because Father kept me in ignorance of His purposes. Satan spoke to me about going back and taking the sheriff's offer, but I fought him off.

"On the third day I found myself in a north and south road, crossed it and found myself in an open lot. Then the other part of the dream was perfectly clear. This was the third room, and I laughed aloud, for now I felt that I was going to be free soon. I crossed the lot and came upon another lot going southwest. Now I knew I was free, so I started off very fast and made thirty-five miles a day for several days."

CHAPTER III.

The story of his dream led to the inquiry as to whether he had other divine revelations through this medium, giving him assurance of future work for him. Francis saw the drift of the question before it was completed, and speaking rapidly, he said: "While I was at Hot Springs I had visions during many nights, In one night I beheld thirty-five. They were like a panorama, following one after another. They showed me clearly events which have already been fulfilled and others yet to come. The work is to be greater. More surprises— greater than those which are known—will come. It may not be for some time and yet it may be only a short time. There are two ways of looking at the time, but I say time will tell. Father uses the simplest way for His work and that is the reason the world will not believe."

Returning to the subject of the visions of his future work, he spoke of their gorgeous nature, but continued: "They are only meant for my eyes, Father does not intend to have them made known. The fulfillment will be wonderful to mankind. Time will tell the story, and they who do not have Faith will be the worse for it."

Continuing the thread of his wanderings, the Healer went southwest through Arkansas, across the southeast corner of the Indian Territory into Texas, bringing up at Paris, Texas, from which point he departed from the Texas and Pacific railway line, healing people when they would listen to him, but in very few instances did he find Faith.

At Throckmorton, Texas, the Healer was again arrested on a charge of vagrancy, brought before a court and sentenced to three days' imprisonment. After serving the judgment he was instructed to leave the town within three days, in lieu of which he was threatened with a long term in jail. It was unnecessary to urge him, for he started at once over what is known as the Llano Estacado or Staked Plains, the northern desert of Texas, arriving at El Paso after enduring great suffering and privation.

He gained El Paso about the first of July, 1894. His route then lay over the sterile, arid Yuma desert, through the extreme southern section of New Mexico, Arizona and southern California. In speaking of the journey, he said that he found the heat intense, but did not suffer for many days. By keeping along the line of the Southern Pacific railroad from El Paso, he was enabled to follow a chain of habitations, where sometimes he was invited to share food, and often went without. Though often fainting from weakness, the Father supported him. After passing the southeastern boundary of California, he fell in with a fellow-traveler who was a tramp, although Francis did not use this term. He said he was a poor fellow like himself, without food or shelter, and who had not the advantage of a trade at which he might work at any time. This nondescript Arab of the wilderness shared with Francis the scanty store, but "misery acquaints a man with strange bedfellows." "He got what I got; we shared alike."

Just outside of Colton, California, these two princes of the wastes put aside their royal rags for the night and prepared to woo the slumber so dearly snatched from the cheerless night.

"I was almost dead. I rolled my trousers into a bundle and placed them under my head for a pillow and soon sank into a sound slumber. During the night the fire at our feet went down, so I got up to gather more wood, and while bending over the coals, trying to get it to burn, my companion made off with my clothes. Then I was in a fix. But he did not get anything for I had nothing. The next day I found clothes near the trail."

On September 25, 1894, Francis arrived at Puente, south of Los Angeles and near Pasadena, where took place his first series of extensive and pronounced healings. Three months and three days were spent in the little San Jacinto valley, passing from town to town, healing many Mexicans and Indians, all of whom were exceedingly grateful. This was the only period during his entire wanderings that the Father commanded him to receive money from those who offered to give it for his work. It came in by dribs of ten, fifteen and twenty cents.

"I did not know what the Father wanted me to take it for, but knew that I should soon discover the reason. The Mexicans and Indians gave me enough to make about $20.

Then Father told me to go to San Diego and take the boat for San Francisco. On my way to San Diego I fell in with another fellow who was without anything and sick of the fever. I healed him and shared what I had with him. We went to San Diego together and took a room. Before getting into bed I began to think of putting my trousers under the mattress. I had given my companion $10 to start into some business in San Diego, finding I could go up by boat for the rest. Father told me to hang my trousers on a hook. It was not for me to question, so I obeyed. When I awoke in the morning I found the money and the man had disappeared, so I had to go out into the country again and raise more. All this time Satan was telling me what an easy time I could have if I only went back to work, but I would not listen.

"Well, I took the boat for San Francisco one month afterwards. I only stayed there six hours. Father told me to leave. I went to San Jose, then over the mountains to Merced, and from here over the mountains to Mojave, was the only ride I had during the journey. I was invited to get on a 'helper' engine. Father told me to ride if I was asked, so I got on. I bought a bag of flour—forty pounds—at Mojave, and, carrying my water with me, started into the Mojave desert in February, 1895. At the Needles my flour had given out. I used to make a paste with the water. At the Needles I got a bag of wheat and ate that with water. Now my real suffering commenced, and Satan was busier than ever before. No man can ever know what I suffered. It was every day, every hour, all the time, and without any rest. Father sometimes took me away from myself."

In answer to whether they were tortures of the flesh or of the mind, he replied: "They were bodily pains that racked me. I did not suffer mentally, because the worse the pains, the happier I grew; but sometimes the suffering was terrible with darkness, and I fought Satan all the time. Nobody has ever suffered like that. Satan would say: 'Throw down those things you carry and go back,' but I would answer: 'No; you cannot make me do as you want as long as Father does not wish it. You cannot lead me astray because Father is with me.' But the vision," he continued, with one of the most joyful, rapt expressions a man could wear—a smile that al-

3

most transfigured him—"Oh, the beautiful,
magnificent visions. One night—it was full
of moonlight and bright as daytime—I saw
the grandest vision ever seen by mortal man.
Sometimes all of the prophets would appear
before me. Sometimes I have seen my mother.
I remember very distinctly. She would comfort me, but often reprove me. Then Father
told me I was ready to begin healing in the
cities. Often I had seen many other visions.
Satan had fled and tempted me no more.

"My feet were on the ground, only the up-
pers of my shoes, so I walked into Flagstaff,
Arizona. I herded sheep there and saw other
visions."

Francis said he procured strips of rubber
and bound them to the soles of his feet to
keep them from being cut on jagged stones.
In his passage across the desert he went for
many days without food or water and con-
tracted a salt famine. When he was given a
bag of salt he was accustomed to dissolve a
quantity of it in his water supply and drink it.
He thought it had a stimulating effect. Those
who befriended him in the slightest way he
declares were blessed.

"Father blessed them in some way," said Francis. "If any one was sick in the family they were made well, though they did not know the cause. I have had the power all along, but people would not believe. 'According to your Faith, so be it with you.' Father takes the simplest ways for his methods, and that is the reason they will not believe. Father was trying me when I was suffering. Father tried Job."

He said the last Bible he had was given to a colored prisoner at Hot Springs; he had carried none in the desert and had none now. When the possibility of disciples was suggested, he shook his head and said: "I do not wish to talk on that. The work will be performed alone for a long time. Greater things are yet to come."

CHAPTER IV.

At Flagstaff, Francis herded sheep for a short time, when the Father ordered him to move on, and he continued his footsteps toward New Mexico. At this time he had a small tent and blankets and was to some extent more comfortable than usual. He arrived at Las Lunas about July 6, 1895. It was at this point that he first attracted public attention. His cures related at this point reached Albuquerque, New Mexico, and it was while here that Mr. Fox heard of him and immediately started to locate him, impressed by something, as he says, which he could not define, that he "must go." While he left Albuquerque for Las Lunas, Francis left Las Lunas for Albuquerque, Mr. Fox meeting him at "Old Town" Albuquerque.

His descriptions of the scenes at Albuquerque are: In a small room and a hallway of an adobe house in "Old Town," the people were packed to suffocation from the time the first rays of the rising sun peeped over the brow of the majestic Sandras until darkness had settled down upon the winding and narrow streets of this ancient village. Francis spent his time with unfailing vigor, though sitting in a room that was hot and stuffy, in an atmosphere heavy and stifling, he ministered to the wants of all those who came to his side. This old fashioned Mexican home was thronged with men and women and children, patiently waiting for those before them to make room for them at the side of the Healer. Men upon whom the weight of years was resting heavily, men in the prime of life and mere boys were there. Old women whose black locks were sprinkled with gray, whose eyes were dim and furrowed, and whose steps were tottering were there. Matrons, bearing in their arms infants, whose eyes have seen the light but a few months and whose tiny faces indicated a struggle for life against the odds of a sweltering summer, were there by hundreds, hoping that the touch of this strange man might bring back the roses to their own cheeks and the light again into baby's eyes. Young girls were there, many

of them out of curiosity, yet all believing in
the man who to them had been proclaimed a
Messiah. The gala day attire of the women
who had done honor to the man by donning
the bright colors so loved by the Spaniards,
lent dashes of color to the otherwise sombre
scene. Without the house was a long line
of wagons and saddle horses, the occupants
and riders of which were waiting their turn
to see Francis.

Into the placita in the rear, and out upon
the wide porch in front, this great crowd over-
flowed, and over all was the hush that bespoke
the awe of the people there. Humbug or not,
these people respected the man of whose kindly
deeds they had heard so much. They knew he
had never done harm; they believed he had
done good. Sprinkled freely throughout the
crowd were many of the best-known and most
respected citizens of New Town. Many of them
were brought there out of curiosity, it is true,
but after they had mingled with the crowd
and had heard of the sublime Faith of the people who had followed him, and the kindly acts
he had performed, they had no harsh words
for him. Many there were, too, who believed in
him; many to whom the man would have done

much-sought favor if he had gone with them,
before he left the city, to the bedside of friends
and relatives who were sick and suffering.
Within the house the Healer sat in a small
apartment before an open window, which
looked out upon the green placita. His well-
shaped head, with the flowing locks, stood out
in bold relief in the square of light. Upon
either side of the chair upon which he sat was
another, and these two were occupied by the
patients. He turned first to one side and then
to the other, when the Healer touched the
hands of the occupants of these seats, and as
his grasp was loosened the patient gave way to
another. Over him stood some kindly senora,
stirring the air into motion with a large fan.
Over and over again the scene was enacted
throughout all the hours of the day, and at
nightfall there were still hundreds before the
door. Stories of cures filled the air. It was
reported by gentlemen whose honesty of purpose cannot be doubted, that a woman of Old
Town whose hand had been paralyzed for
years found full use of it after she had touched
the hands of the Healer. Also, that a man
who had been lame for years found himself
fully recovered after being treated. One man,

whose baby had been touched by Francis, declared that the infant had been cured of a high
fever, which raged so the day before that the
little one's life had been despaired of.

CHAPTER V.

On the 23d day of July, 1895, standing bare-headed under the rays of a fierce, burning sun, at the same place, was Francis Schlatter, while between 400 and 600 persons pushed and shoved to obtain a position of advantage. One by one the crowd of sickly and infirm persons passed before him, and to each some kind word was spoken or an inaudible prayer was offered up. Grasping the hand of those who were most infirm, and holding them long enough to appeal for a cure, most of the day went by.

One of the most dramatic incidents of this day occurred after Francis had left the little room in the adobe and was standing out in the spacious porch in front. It was announced that all who cared to could shake hands with him. As he stood there a long line was formed and passed before him. While the people passed and there were many who had not reached him, four Zuni Indians were seen advancing, bearing among them a sick brave, whose step was uncertain and whose eyes had nearly been put out, it seemed from their appearance, by an explosion of powder.

Francis saw them advancing and he waved the crowd back, that room might be made for them. When the Indians reached him, all threw themselves upon the ground at his feet, prostrate before the man in whom their Faith was boundless. "Don't prostrate yourselves before me," said Francis, in their own language; "I want none to kneel to me." Still the Indians lay at his feet, and he took each by the hand and raised him up. In the center of the group stood the sightless Indian, his eyes swollen and inflamed. Schlatter grasped him by the hands. The sightless Zuni's efforts to see the Healer's face were pitiful in the extreme. His upturned face showed the anguish he felt, and a quick motion of the head, as though to force open the sightless eyes, indicated the emotion which stirred his breast. Dropping the Indian's hands, Francis passed his hands over the patient's eyes, and there are witnesses who declare solemnly the inflammation had gone down after the touch. Schlatter informed the Indian he would have to take several treatments Early in the afternoon of the same day a man informed Francis that he was badly needed at Barelas, and asked him if he would go there. There was a large crowd before him at the time, and, motioning the crowd back, he answered that he would inform the messenger in a moment.

Down upon his knees he went, his face turned up toward the bright blue skies above him. His lips moved as if in prayer, and those near him heard the soft cadence of the voice, not quite a whisper, not quite above it. Rising from his knees, Schlatter answered that he would go in an hour and a half from that time.

When the time came for him to go, there was a wild scramble to see who should have the honor of carrying him to his destination. Men unhitched teams which did not belong to them and fought for the place of honor. Some idea of the veneration in which this man was held by the people who had gathered around him in Old Town may be understood from an incident which occurred the day before. An American who approached the outskirts of the crowd was asked by some one if he had seen the man about whom all had gathered. "No; where is the — —?" was the reply. Scores of men in the crowd heard it, and the glances from the dark eyes cast upon the speaker were full of threatening light. The man understood and hastily left. For several days there was much talk about causing the arrest of Francis. When this was learned, one of the most prominent Spanish citizens of Albuquerque, one who had visited the Werner home and had seen the people who had gathered there for the last two days, said: "There is not a large enough police force in Bernalillo county to arrest this man when he is in the midst of a crowd. Any one who would lay hands on him would be torn to pieces. I know these people. I know how deeply they are wrought up over this matter, and I know what they would do." Nearly every man, woman and child in Bernalillo county knows Perfecto Armijo, and he is also well known in all parts of New Mexico, and no one who knows him will for a moment doubt the truth of any statement he makes.

Mr. Armijo was questioned as to whether he knew anything about the Healer, and he said:

"Yes, I have been over there, and stayed for some time. There is a great crowd around him of people who have come from all parts of the surrounding country to be treated by him. He

treats rich and poor, high and low, with perfect impartiality, and makes no charge for anything he does." "But," said another man, "did
you learn of any good that he has done to any
one, or is he, as some say, only a fake?" "I
heard of a great many," said Mr. Armijo, "who
claimed to have been benefited by him." "But
is there any case in which, to your personal
knowledge, he has done any good?" "There
are a number of cases," said he, "that have
come to me on such reliable authority that I
have no reason to doubt them; but there is
only one of which I can speak from my own
personal knowledge." "Well, as to that one;
have you any objections to telling what it is?"
"No objections at all," said he; "but, on
the contrary, I am glad to let it be known. My
wife's mother, Mrs. Conception Garcia, has for
many years past had a paralyzed arm, and was
not able to make any more use of it than if it
had been amputated. When she heard of this
man she determined to go and see him. We
tried to dissuade her from it, because none of
the rest of us had any confidence in him. We
told her that he was merely a 'crazy humbug,'
traveling around the country and deceiving the
ignorant classes, and that if she ran after him

she would simply make herself ridiculous and cause people to laugh at her for her credulity.

"But, notwithstanding all our protests, she was determined to go, and so, to humor her, I had the carriage brought and took her over to Old Town.

"Well, she worked her way through the crowd and went in and saw him, and when she came out she had just as good use of the paralyzed arm as she had of the other one, and is working around the house at this very hour, with just as good use of both her arms as any other woman of her age in the country. That's all I know about the man, but that's enough to change my opinion of him. A fact like that, coming right home to me in my own house, doesn't admit of any argument or leave room for any doubt."

Mariano Armijo, who was among the doubters before Francis came to Albuquerque, spent an evening with the Healer since his arrival in Albuquerque, and his account of it is very interesting: "We sat in the room with this man after the crowd had gone for the day," he said. "The only patient present was a blind man, who had come down from Denver to be treated. As the man held the blind man's hands in his own, the Healer talked to us, telling of his experiences and his travels. The tale was an interesting one and the time passed rapidly. I should judge a half hour passed before he dropped the blind man's hands. As he did so the blind man sank back in his chair, evidently exhausted. He cried out for air, and complained of the extreme heat of the room. I looked at him and noticed he was dripping with perspiration. It was evening at the time, and none of the rest of us felt warm in the least. One of my acquaintances," continued Mr. Armijo, "whom I have known positively to have been hardly able to walk at all, met me on the street to-day. He was on the opposite corner when I heard him cry out to me. I turned in the direction from which the voice came and saw this acquaintance waving his hat in the air and running toward me as nimble as a boy. He was perfectly happy and said he could walk as well as he ever could. I have known personally of his affliction for years."

Tereso Ulevini, who was lame for years, said that he had been treated by the Healer, and that he had been greatly improved. "I have been lame for years. At night I had such excruciating pains in my thighs that I have been unable to get any rest for nights at a time. Many nights my wife has been up with me a dozen times. I went to this man and for the last two nights I have had absolutely no pain and have slept like a child. I do not pretend to understand it, but I know I have been benefited."

Mr. Will Hunter, of Albuquerque, wrote as follows regarding the Healer:

CHAPTER VI.

Wonderfully like the story of the Scriptures as rehearsed in the New Testament is the tale upon every lip in the central part of New Mexico to-day. Wonderfully like the scenes of the Bible, in setting and in some of the characters, have been the scenes enacted here.

Here in New Mexico there suddenly burst into view, whence no one seems to know, a man bearing a striking resemblance to the pictures of the Christ who looked upon just such scenes as these nearly 1,900 years ago; a man who tastes not of food; a man whose touch is said to bring sight to the blind, hearing to the deaf, motion to the halt, peace to the suffering. Like the Christ he was first doubted by these people, though he came among them professing to be no more than he appeared. Like the Christ he won his followers by his kindly deeds, his cure of the afflicted, his unselfish devotion to mankind. Like the Christ he was persecuted, the higher class of the Mexican population threatening

4

him as an imposter, a sharper, a schemer, a
lunatic, and his persecutors he transformed
into his staunchest friends.

For more than two weeks he has been followed by hundreds wherever he has gone. To-
day a constant stream of people passed before
him, praying that he touch their hands. Blind,
deaf and halt are led or carried to him, women
with tiny babies bring them to him to be
healed of ailments, real or imaginary; old,
young, middle aged, ignorant and educated
Mexicans, Americans of the highest standing
in the community, visit him at the lowly homes
he most frequents or in the homes of the rich
and prominent in which he is a welcome guest.
Great lines of carriages, and wagons and saddle horses stand before every house he enters,
the owners, drivers or riders having come for
him to take him to the house of some one who
is suffering. Each and all, high or lowly, he
treats the same and from no one will he take
a cent for the services he has performed,
though money has been repeatedly pressed
upon him. To all he has the same kindly greeting, the same kindly treatment.

Stories of his cures are beyond belief. Many
of them have been investigated and now even

the most credulous are willing to admit the man has done many men good and no man harm; that he is honest in his endeavors to aid suffering humanity and consistent in his actions. As to whence comes his power opinions differ. Among the Mexicans few doubt it comes direct from heaven; among the Americans it is attributed to animal magnetism and the principles upon which the Christian Science doctrine is founded.

Monday afternoon, July 15, a Mexican attache of the morning newspaper in this city rushed breathlessly into the office, his face the picture of amazement. The day previous he had been at Peralta, a small town down the Rio Grande river, about twenty miles south of this city. There, he said, he had seen a man who was the perfect picture of the prints of the Christ which adorn the walls of the ancient cathedral of San Felipe, the towers of which have been outlined against the sky for more than 300 years. This man had been surrounded all day by crowds of people; he had held the hands of a blind man and sight had been restored to the patient; he had touched the hands of a woman who had been paralyzed for years and she left as well as in the days of her maidenhood; he had treated many others and all have been benefited. Since his advent into that village, in a miraculous manner seven days before, it was known he had not tasted food.

All this the Mexican breathlessly and hurridly related. His word being doubted he offered to take his incredulous listeners to the man. While all appeared too improbable to be given the slightest attention, the newspaper instinct prevailed and the next morning, before the sun had peeped over the mountains, the Mexican as driver and guide, the writer and two others started off on a "fool's errand" toward Peralta.

On the way everyone met was asked about this strange man, whom no one save the driver expected to see. Each person asked seemed to know who was meant, and in an indefinite way something of his whereabouts. All spoke of his strange appearance and of the wonderful things he had done.

At Peralta, the wagon stopped before a house from which stepped an old Mexican, walking as nimbly as a boy. In his hand he carried a cane, though he made no use of it. That he was blind no one thought for a moment. As he talked it became known that he was the blind man whose sight it was alleged had been restored. In simple language Jesus Valesquez told his story:

"For three years," he said, "I have not seen my hand before me. I have tried many physicians for my blindness, but none was able to help me. A few days ago this man came to town and I went to him. He took my hands in his, my right in his left, my left in his right, and as he held them he mumbled something to himself. After I left him my sight began to come back. I could tell when the lamp was lighted at night. Soon I could see the light. Gradually my sight came back until now I am able to see quite plainly objects not far away."

Every possible test was made upon the old man to discover if he could see. In all he proved beyond question that his eyesight was fairly good.

"Where did this man come from and what is his name?" was asked.

"No one knows his name," answered the Mexican. "His coming was strange indeed. Some boys went to the top of that black mountain there to play and there they found this man lying flat upon his back with his arms stretched up towards heaven. Beside him was a small, tepee-shaped tent and outside this was a couch of blankets. They ran from him in terror and the man followed them to the village."

Further down the road the wagon stopped at the house of Silverio Martino, a well known resident of Peralta. Asked about the Healer, for that seemed to be the only name by which this strange man was known, Martino said he had stopped there while in Peralta and had left there his tent and staff. Proudly he conducted his callers to a little room of the adobe house where he had carefully put away a small, tepee-shaped tent and a stick, evidently cut from a fence board, about twelve feet long, bound in places with bits of wire or thongs of leather, the ends cut arrow-shaped. Martino declared he had watched his guest night and day, being relieved by one of his family while he slept, and that he would take oath the Healer had not tasted food in several days. Asked what good this man had done, Martino said his mother, Juliana Sedillo, had been paralyzed in her left arm so that she could not lift it from her side, for sixteen years; that the Healer had touched her and that she was then at work in the field.

Out in the field was found an old Mexican woman, working away as though with great delight, handling her rude implement of agriculture as well as any of those near her.

Not being able to question the fact the man could see or the woman had full use of her arms, the investigators began an inquisition to discover whether the man had really been blind or the woman paralyzed. Everyone met with declared such to have been the case. Finally Don Andreas Romero, a highly educated Spaniard and one of the best known men in the territory, was found, and he declared he personally knew that Valesquez had not been able to see for three years or the woman to use her arm for sixteen years. Don Romero also stated that it was known beyond question the man had not tasted food since he had been in the village.

Through Valencia, across the Rio Grande by ford, with water up to the top of the buggy seats, through Los Lunas and a number of other villages, the Healer was followed, and strange stories of his doings were added at every mile. At the Indian pueblo of Isleta it was learned that the man had been there several hours before and that he had gone to Pajarito.

At Pajarito, in the small parlor of the adobe house of Juan Garcia, sat the man whom the credulous information-seekers had followed nearly fifty miles.

He is a man of about six feet in height and weighs probably 160 pounds. His form is that of the athlete and like the athlete he has all the supple grace of the man of trained muscles.

First of all to strike the observer is the remarkable likeness between him and the pictures of Christ. The long flowing brown hair, curling slightly at the shoulders over which it spread, the brown beard falling gracefully upon the breast, the small white patches devoid of hair just at the corners of the mouth, which mark the perfect Jewish facial adornment, were all there. The eyes, blue and clear as the sky without, beamed with a most kindly light upon all who approached. The mouth, firm and delicately cut, was faintly seen between the beard and the mustache. As long as the mouth was closed the resemblance between the man and a picture of Christ which adorned one of the walls of the room, was complete; when the lips parted the illusion was shattered, for the absence of two teeth from the upper jaw robbed the face of its striking appearance. For clothing the man wears simply a blue calico shirt, a blue jeans "jumper" falling over the hips to meet blue overalls, much too short and not meeting a pair of cheap socks which covered the feet. No hat, no shoes, though the sands of New Mexico are blistering and the sun intensely hot.

First to apply to him for the healing touch was a relative of the host, an old man who had totally lost the sight of one eye. Motioning him to a seat the Healer took the hands of the patient in his own. For five minutes the two sat there speechless. The lips of the Healer could be seen to move from time to time and occasionally his big blue eyes were directed upward. Now and then, too, a shudder seemed to pass over him, his body swaying with the emotion. The old man's sightless orb was directed toward the face of the man to whom he had come for succor and his body swayed with the emotion of anticipation. They sat there speechless until, with a sigh,

the old man arose and went out into the
placita.

Men, women and children took the seat he
had vacated, and the former proceeding was
repeated. Some left the chair declaring that
the pain had vanished; others said they had
noticed no beneficial results. As the Healer
held the hands of his patients, he talked with
the people.

"Do you heal by the Christian Science
method?"

"I know no science; I simply do as I am
told."

"What percentage of cures do you effect?"

"I don't know. I treat all who come to
me and never think of them after they leave."

Just at that moment the wife of a prominent
Mexican asked Schlatter if he would come to
her home. Schlatter's eyes were turned upward and after a moment, during which he
seemed to be praying, he said:

"I will go one week from to-day, at noon."

"Where will you be at that time?"

"Only my Master knows. But wherever I
am, if you send a messenger for me I will come
at that time."

An hour afterwards, just as a storm crept in from the mountains, he started for the Indian village of Isleta.

The publication of the facts as given above, without their being colored in the slightest, caused such a commotion as Albuquerque has not seen in years. The newspaper giving the account was subjected to the most severe criticism. Among the leading Mexicans of the city the feeling against the paper was particularly strong. The editor was visited in the office for several days by prominent Mexicans, who accused him of trying to make out that the natives of this territory are more ignorant, more gullible and more superstitious than the people of other sections of the country. The article was considered by these gentlemen as a direct attack upon the Mexican population and it was confidently asserted by these callers that not one iota of foundation could be found for the report. Among the Americans the story was laughed at as a sensational fabrication and few persons believed at first there was any such man to be found.

Many there were, however, who did believe the accounts, and who took pains to ascertain if there were any foundation to be found. Peo-

ple, too, began dropping in from the neighbor-
hood in which the man was reported to have
been and the tales they told were even more
strange than any that had been printed. The
news spread rapidly and in a few days a blind
man came from Denver to be treated. With a
guide he spent Saturday scouring the country
for him, but to no purpose.

Sunday morning Schlatter appeared in Albuquerque, at the home of Mrs. Werner, in
that portion of the city called Old Town.

The news of his arrival spread through the
city like wildfire, and from the moment of his
arrival early Sunday morning until late that
night, hundreds of people were struggling to
get to his side. Not for years have such
crowds gathered as were there that Sunday
and during the seven days following that
Schlatter has been in this city. Men upon
whom the weight of years was resting heavily;
men in the prime of life; mere boys, followed
him. Old women, whose black locks were
sprinkled with gray, whose eyes were dim and
whose cheeks were furrowed, followed him.
Matrons bearing in their arms infants whose
eyes have scarce seen the light and whose tiny
faces indicate the terrible struggle against

the odds of a sweltering summer, followed him
by hundreds, hoping that a touch of this
strange man's hand might bring back the roses
to their cheeks and the light to the children's
eyes. Young girls followed him. All were
dressed in gala attire, the bright colors so much
affected by the Spaniards lending dashes of
color to the otherwise somber scene.

At first few persons but the Mexicans went
to him for treatment. As stories from the
lips of the patients themselves filled the air,
the more highly educated Spaniards and the
Americans began looking into the matter.
Every day the Healer made converts, and men
who had decried him as an imposter publicly
apologized for their unbelief and their unkind
remarks. The Healer began yielding to the
pleadings of some of the most wealthy citizens
who desired him to go to their homes until,
when it became generally known he would go
when asked, he has been the guest of some
of the most prominent citizens of Albuquerque. All admitted there was something
remarkable about the man. All admired him
for his honesty of purpose and endeavor, and
all admitted he did much good.

Many of the leading people of the city were

among his patients, and the result of their treatment was watched by the entire city. One prominent citizen promised to build Schlatter a church if his wife be cured of an affliction.

In spite of the laudation given him, in spite of the fact he is eagerly sought by the rich and influential, Schlatter's manner did not change in the least.

He treated all alike, and seemed not to know or see the person he grasped by the hand.

Though money and clothing have been offered him by hundreds of people, he was never known, save in one instance, to take anything tendered. That one exception occurred at Tome, a small town near Peralta. A man whom he had cured insisted upon his taking money, but Schlatter persistently refused until it was seen refusals would do no good. Then he stretched out his hand for the money. Receiving it, he turned to a number of poor people who were about him and divided it among them.

"I have no use for money," was all he said.

Most remarkable about him, perhaps, was that he partook of no solid food. For seventeen days he was watched by men of repute, who were willing to take oath he put nothing into his stomach in that time except water.

Still another phase of the case which attracted much comment was the clairvoyant power of the man. Numerous instances were cited where the man foretold calls that would be made upon him when the caller him-self was still among the skeptics and had no idea of going. He foretold, too, occurrences of every-day business life which affected him when there was no possible chance of his know-ing aught of the subject-matter.

Converts to this strange man's cause, of course, have not been made without some rea-son for it. This something has been his cure of people of all classes.

Charles Slamp, whose foot had been crushed by a railroad car, said:

"About two hours after I had been treated by this man, after I had been carried home, being unable to bear the least weight on the in-jured foot, and not knowing why, I jumped out of bed, alighting squarely on it. Since then I have been able to walk upon it without pain."

Mrs. C. Oxendine, wife of a well-known ex-pressman of this city, was almost helpless with rheumatism. She was treated by Schlatter, and since, her husband states, she has been as well as she ever was in her life.

Peter H. McGuire, of Winslow, who was so badly affected with rheumatism that he had to walk with two crutches, threw both away after he had visited the Healer. Since he has had no return of the trouble.

C. J. Roentgen, of Denver, says his wife, who was stone deaf before she was treated by Schlatter, is now able to carry on a conversation in ordinary conversational tones.

These are but samples of the tales which are repeated by hundreds in this city. Whether any of the so-called cures will prove permanent remains to be seen.

Some of the opinions of the man among the people who have studied him are of interest:

Walter C. Hadley is probably the wealthiest man in this city. He is an ex-territorial senator and ex-editor. He is prominently connected with all the advanced movements in the city and of the territory and the Southwest. In order to study Schlatter, he invited him to his home. After his guest had gone, Mr. Hadley said:

"This much I will say for him: He is not an imposter. He is just what he represents him-

self to be. He is consistent in all his actions.
That he has power I cannot deny, since I have
been treated by him. Whence it comes I cannot say. That he has the power of animal magnetism to a wonderful degree cannot be denied.
The science of psychic force is still in its infancy. Whether these things explain it all I
cannot say. Such power as he has must work
for good, and when the possessor, who or what
he may be, gives it freely for the benefit of
mankind, receiving for its exercise no portion
of this world's worldly goods, he should not be
discouraged by intelligent persons in any walk
of life."

Don Tomas Guiterrez, who for years has held
the position of probate court judge here, and
who was one of the indignant doubters from
the first, says:

"I do not pretend to explain it, but the fact
is this man is doing many very wonderful
things and is accomplishing much good. This
is so plain to any one who will take the trouble
to investigate, that it would be idle for any
one to deny it. I am not in any manner superstitious, but I have seen enough to convince
my judgment."

5

CHAPTER VII.

Through the instrumentality of Mr. Fox, who visited the Healer at Albuquerque, he was induced to come to Denver. Pursuant to that understanding, Francis left Albuquerque on the evening of the 21st day of August, 1895, arriving in Denver the morning of the 23d. His coming had been heralded by the newspapers and a great mass of humanity beseiged the private residence in North Denver. All were anxious for a glimpse of Francis Schlatter, the "second Messiah," the Healer, as he was called. To all admittance was denied. After his forty days' fast, the man who had grown suddenly famous insisted upon three weeks of perfect quiet. Some came with full Faith that ailments that baffled physicians would be cured by the laying on of hands. Hundreds went out of curiosity only. Stretched upon a couch in the home of a man who regarded his strange guest with the utmost reverence, surrounded by dainties to tempt his appetite, looking from sky-blue

E. I. Fox, with whom the Healer lived in Denver.

eyes which flashed a kindly light, with parted lips, smiling, an intellectual countenance, laid a man who has attracted wide attention within the past months. As to his personality, his lips were sealed. To the direct question, "Are you the Christ?" he answers, "I am."

Without the question he made no pretense as to who or what he was. Whatever may be the views of the individual as to Francis Schlatter, no one who conversed with him will deny that he was a person of wonderful magnetism, that he has supreme Faith in his mission, that he thoroughly believed that he was sent by One above, and that he was commissioned to heal the sick. The most noticeable thing to the visitor was the perfect, child-like simplicity of the man. There was no argument from him. The whole tenor of his speech was that no proof was needed. The man left his work to tell the story. The skeptical asked him what proof he had that he was the Christ. The only answer was that his works of healing showed that he was on earth for that purpose.

The incredulous left the couch with the conviction that while the claim that this human being was sent to do wonders may be untrue, there could be no possible doubt that Francis Schlatter believed that he had been selected to perform what seemed to be miracles. There was a strange light in the eye, there was a directness and earnestness in the speech that left no room for the conclusion that his invalid was a fakir. He made no effort to conceal anything. He told the visitor that he had nothing to say as to who he was. When the question was asked him as to whether he was the Christ, he said it was his duty to answer. No amount of twisting or modifying the purport of what he said changed the answer, which always was, "I am." If he possessed no power, if his control over physical weakness was a myth, the Faith that predominated the words and the acts of the man impressed one. His confidence in his ability to perform anything that the Father wished done was the mastering thought and the one thing that caused the scoffer to hold his tongue. It would seem sacrilegious to deny a conclusion in which the man had such an evident abiding Faith.

Some said there had been an attempt on the part of Francis to conform his appearance to some of the later ideas on this subject. He certainly had an intellectual countenance, and the

hair, growing long and wavy, made a striking
resemblance to some of the pictures extant of
the Great Healer. Before Francis had left the
Union hotel (his first stopping place on his arrival in Denver), he had many callers. This
was at 7 o'clock in the morning, and before
noon the hotel clerk had directed at least 300
people to the home of ex-Alderman E. L. Fox,
in North Denver, where it was supposed the
visitor would stop. These invalids made haste
to this address, but all were disappointed.
Francis had gone to the residence of Harry
Hauenstein, 336 Fairview avenue. The crowd
was again doomed to failure in the attempt to
reach the man who was believed to possess the
power to heal. At the door all were informed
that Schlatter could not be seen. They went
away sorrowfully, the halt and the blind. It
was a motley assembly that beseiged the door
of the cottage all day long. The blind owner
told the visitors that for the present the Healer
must have absolute quiet. Many suffered from
rheumatism, from palsy, from all manner of
diseases, as well as bereft of sight, and begged
in vain for an audience with the man whose
fame had gone abroad from the quiet little
Mexican village. When a paper man appeared

at the cottage, he was made welcome. The only thing to be determined was as to whether he really was a reporter. This fact being demonstrated, he was admitted to the parlor, where he found Francis lying upon a couch. "I knew you were coming," said the man, with a smile. "How is that?" he was asked. "O," he replied, "the Father told me so." The second Messiah was evidently very weak physically. A basket of peaches and grapes was upon the chair. There was a tumbler of ice water at his side also. "Fill this, please," he said to Mr. Hauenstein. "Water is the best thing, after all. Then I want to talk for a few minutes." He said that he was very weak, and had determined that he would see no one for at least three weeks. His fast of forty days and forty nights had left him decidedly enfeebled. The arms were thin, being almost devoid of flesh. There were no symptoms of disease, but he looked weak. The skin, usually of dark color, had become white.

His long hair was here and there tinged with gray, a smile made the features interesting. Francis has a well-formed mouth and his long teeth, made prominent by a short upper lip, did not detract from his striking appearance. It was impossible to describe the peculiar light that shined from his bright blue eyes. Though pale, the face had an intellectual and not unhealthy look. He chose to tell what he had to say in his own way, and spoke with few interruptions. He said that his appetite had not been good since the long fast. He had suffered greatly on the journey from Albuquerque.

"It would have driven any man crazy," said Francis. "But," he added, with a smile, "I know I have to go through this suffering."

"What is there about this claim that you are the Christ?" asked in an anxious mind.

"I never claimed that I was the Christ," responded Francis. "My mission is to heal. When the question is put straight to me I have to answer it. Otherwise I never say a word."

"Are you the Christ?" asked the same individual.

"I am," promptly responded Francis.

"But what proof have you of the fact? How do you pretend to say that you are Christ, the Son of God?"

"I have plenty of proof that I am the Christ," he responded. "Four have seen the proof. Three of them are Mexicans. I have proven I am Christ by my works. The Father does not want the work done instantly. Some people say, 'If you are the Christ, why don't you cure instantly?' The Father does not want it that way. The blind will see and the deaf will hear, though."

This last statement was made in an assuring and calm tone, and as though that matter was finally and irrevocably settled.

"And there will be a stranger effect here than in Albuquerque," he continued. "But it will never be instantly.

"What would be the use of giving proof, anyway," he mused, dreamily. "They wouldn't believe it because they wouldn't understand. I don't ask them to believe. If they ask me the question I have to answer. If they don't believe me, that's their own business."

"What do you mean by saying that the effect will be stronger in Denver than in Albuquerque?"

"Because," he replied, "the Father tells me so. It is not I that does the healing, but the Father. Now, I will not see anyone for three weeks. But it doesn't make any difference. I don't need to see a person. Just a waste of time for all these people who have wanted to get to see me to-day to be cured. People coming here to see me can't see me. The mere fact of their coming is enough. The Father puts a force at work that will cure them. For instance, in New Mexico, a party wrote me a letter from Santa Fe, asking when he could see me to be healed. The letter was not mailed, but the party began to grow better. The letter was handed me some time after it was written. That wish to be cured set the force at work.

"The Father gives me power," he said, "else I have nothing. With Him I can do all things. If He doesn't want me to heal I can't heal. I must do His wish and will in the smallest particular and in this I never failed."

Here the speaker's voice grew solemn and eloquent. The broken German accent, the low spoken words made the scene impressive as he continued:

"No matter what was ahead of me, when He told me to go I went; when He told me to stay I stayed; when He told me to lay by the roadside for days, I remained there."

"As I understand you, what you mean to say is not that you are really Christ, the Son of God, but that you possess from the Father a power that is not given to other men?"

"In answer to your question as to whether I was the Christ I said, ' I am,' " replied Francis, quietly. "That is the answer Jesus Christ gave. He is the Father. I am the Son. Only the power that the Father gives, do I have.

"Ryan has slept with me two nights," he said, "he knows he's a hundred per cent. better."

Francis said that he would rest for three weeks; he did not care who came.

"These people can just as well stay at home," he declared. "If they only wish in good Faith to be cured, the Father will cure them without seeing me. If they get mad they lose more than they make. That don't trouble me. If the Father wanted me to work, I would be at work."

Francis announced that he was very weak and needed rest. While his form was considerably emaciated, Francis had not the appearance of suffering from any wasting disease. His cheeks, although paler than usual, had a ruddy glow, and when he talked one did not even notice the pallor. He spoke with a German accent and his words, though spoken slowly, were at times very difficult to understand correctly, but at the slightest intimation that the visitor did not follow his language, he at once repeated what he had said.

CHAPTER VIII.

The evening of his first day in Denver he appeared very weak, so much so that Mr. Fox was alarmed about his condition, which the Healer seemed to notice, and in a reassuring tone he said: "Don't worry; I will be better in the morning," and true to his saying, he was a new man in the morning, all pain having left him, and he appeared to have gained twenty pounds in weight. From that time on until he began public treatment, he grew strong and well.

The beginning of his work in Denver is thus described by the Rocky Mountain News:

After a short rest, Francis Schlatter, the New Mexican Messiah, emerged from his seclusion. Persons in search of this strange Healer had no difficulty in locating the spot he had chosen for his work. All day a steady stream of humanity poured through North Denver toward the cottage of Mr. E. L. Fox, of 625 Witter street, where the Healer made his home. The stream gathered in front of

the neat little wooden residence. Leaning
with one hand against the front fence, stood
a benign faced man with long hair falling over
his shoulders. The Healer wore no coat, and
during all the weary hours from 9 o'clock in
the morning till 4 o'clock in the afternoon he
spoke but few words. His lips moved as if
in prayer. Occasionally he cast his eyes upward, but at all times there was an expression
of peaceful happiness upon his countenance.

The Healer always stopped a short time for
rest at noon. The crowd continued to gather,
and when he appeared at the front door of
the cottage there were fully 1,500 persons oc-
cupying the pavement and the street. Every
nationality was represented in the throng.
The blind, the lame and the deaf were there,
and scores of persons afflicted with rheumatism appeared during the afternoon. Many
came to see, and after their curiosity was satisfied they retired and wondered what manner
of man it was that thus gave his strength and
his time without money and without price for
the benefit of his fellow-beings. Some persons of both sexes seemed strangely infatu-
ated with the Messiah. They stood for hours
and looked steadily into his face, and even

after Francis retired from his arduous task, many lingered, as if they stood on sacred ground. Before dark the crowd melted away. but they left a great pile of handkerchiefs, which Francis was supposed to take into his hands and bless. Several hundred handkerchiefs were treated by Schlatter each day and distributed back to their owners. It was estimated that the total number of handkerchiefs reached more than 1,000 the first day. This was about the number of persons who clasped the hands of the Healer. After the first day the distribution of handkerchiefs took place but twice a day, at 10 o'clock in the morning and at 4:30 in the afternoon.

It was the desire of the Healer that each person that applied for treatment should leave a handkerchief, to be afterwards used in home treatment. A large clothes basket was filled with the handkerchiefs left over from the first day, to be distributed the following forenoon.

The method of treatment followed by Francis has been described and is well known. He took the patient by both hands and grasped firmly for periods that varied, according to the severity of the ailment. The column passed by the Healer at the rate of three persons a

minute. Many of the men took off their hats
as they approached the silent individual, who
received the millionaire and the pauper upon
an equal footing. Ladies dressed in the rich-
est silks stood in line with the wives and children of Italian gardeners. Men who have held
responsible offices in the county and city were
seen in the column. "We are all the children
of one Father," was a favorite expression of the
Healer. An affecting scene was the presenta-
tion of an afflicted lady who was brought late
to the Healer. The patient was brought to the
spot in a carriage. Effort was made by her
friends to induce Francis to leave the place
and treat the invalid in the carriage. The press
was so great that they could not approach near
enough to make their wants known. After
they had waited an hour or more, the assistance of strong arms was secured and the patient was lifted and carried to the
Healer. Her wan face and sunken eyes
told of suffering unto death. Even the
most skeptical person in the crowd bowed
his or her head in silence as Schlatter
solemnly performed the act which he said has
never yet failed to bring relief. A blind man
came next. "I have traveled 360 miles to feel

the grasp of your hands," was his greeting, as
the strong clasp of Francis closed over his fingers. This was one of the few moments when
Schlatter broke his usual silence. "Your sight
will be restored within three months," said the
Healer; "have Faith." Next came a mining
man of Georgetown, of this state. "About a
month ago I received a letter from Mr. Schlatter, in reply to one which I had written," said
Mr. D. M. Powers. "He told me to use the letter to cure my pains. For two years I had been
afflicted with rheumatism, and had reached
such a stage that I prayed for death every day.
All medicine failed and I gave up hope, until
I heard of the cures made by the Healer in New
Mexico. I tried the effect of laying the letter
on the spots that pained me most. I grew better and was well within a month. One month
previous I could not walk. Now I can strike
quite a gait." The Georgetown man was accompanied by two other companions in pain,
who returned home confident that their cure
was effected. One of the men was affected
with rheumatism, and the other with deafness.

Mr. Fox gathered the handkerchiefs as they
poured in. He was assisted by two other gentlemen. A big black dog that belonged on the

6 O'Clock A. M. Waiting for the Healer.

premises sat in the rear of the yard and barked at the strangers as they gathered in front of the house. People rode up in carriages, took a long look at the Healer, and then rode away. The women were visibly affected at the strange scene. A very pretty little woman, whose appearance gave the impression of perfect health, came up. She looked at Francis very curiously as he held her delicate white hands in his broad palms. Then came an intelligent-looking man of fifty-five or sixty years. He was dressed in a fine suit of black, and his bearing indicated that he was a minister of the gospel or a lawyer. He gave no indication of the effect of the personal contact with the silent and mysterious personage. A woman with an expression of pain on her face next occupied the attention of Francis. This patient evidently had exhausted the known remedies for her ailment, and she prayed devoutedly as she stood for a minute before the Healer. The next was D. K. Tammany, a well-known Denver man, who held up his arm, which was stiff. A few minutes after he said: "I have suffered from a stiffness in my right wrist for six years. It was impossible for me to bend my wrist or to move my thumb. See what I can do now."

6

The man bent his wrist without apparent effort. He called attention to a moisture which had appeared on his hand, and remarked that he had noticed nothing of the kind for years.

One of the happiest men in Denver on that day was W. C. Dillon. "Inflammatory rheumatism, with gout symptoms, was my trouble," said he. "I have suffered the tortures of hades for two years, but I feel that half my pains are already gone. When Mr. Schlatter first grasped my hand I could not close my fingers. Within a minute I was able to grasp harder than he. When I reached this spot I could not move a joint. Now all my joints are flexible."

An Indian mother and two comely daughters appeared and were treated. The mother and daughters looked in absolutely perfect health, the daughters being two of the handsomest women on the grounds during that day.

"When He sends it, I have it. When He does not send it, I do not have it. It all depends upon what He sends. God is the giver of all things." These were the words of Francis in reply to a question from a man in the crowd. While the Healer spoke the work of treatment continued without cessation. At times Francis sighed, but not from weakness. He said he never felt stronger in his life. An old woman occupied a place in front of the Healer for a long time during the day. She seemed to be engaged in prayer, and little noticed the stream that passed along. At last she was given opportunity to clasp the hand of Francis. She retired one or two paces and held her hands together, as if in the attitude of supplication or adoration. The eyes of the Healer fell upon the poor woman. "By and by it will be all right," said Francis, in an assuring tone of voice. "In seven months it will be all right." The woman said nothing in reply, but the expression of gladness that smoothed out her wrinkled face transformed her again to the years of youth.

After the Healer retired to the house he talked freely upon his work. "It's day and night work," said he. "The mail this morning brought me many letters, and the afternoon mail has not yet arrived. I try to answer every letter. The Father gives me strength." The handkerchiefs were brought in and Francis treated a big basket full of them as he talked. Mr. Fox came into the room with his daughter, who had just returned from school. Miss Fox was afflicted with deafness, but stated that under treatment of the Healer her trouble had almost disappeared. "I am acting under the will of the Father," said Francis, "and will continue to treat all that come until the 16th of November, when I shall take a rest of two weeks. I am always happy," said Francis, in reply to a remark that he seemed so cheerful; "just as happy in a jail as in a palace. I have no need of money; it would be only a trouble. When Father wants me to get anything, I get it. I do His will. It is all healing now. I never preach." "Mr. Schlatter," inquired a listener, "what do you say when you pray?" "I pray the Lord's prayer," was the response; "it is enough. You may use forms of your own, but the Lord's prayer is all I use."

The Healer talked at length concerning his experiences of the past two years. He said he liked to study geometry, but had little taste for books. He read the Bible when he got a chance, but he was reading the Old Testament, especially the chapters written by the prophets. "I couldn't read the Bible in jail," said Francis; "they wouldn't let me have a Bible there." This was in Hot Springs, Arkansas.

A young man succeeded in gaining an entrance into the room and was treated for crooked eyes. Francis told him his eyes would be straightened in two months, and advised him to wear a handkerchief on his chest day and night. "It will make you a better man all over," said he, as he handed a handkerchief to the patient.

The crowd seemed hungry to gain a sight of the Healer again, and Mr. Fox and his wife had great difficulty in preventing the throng from pushing its way through the front and back doors. From the experiences of the first day, the hosts of Francis expressed a fear that they would not be able to endure the strain of the two months that were to follow.

CHAPTER IX.

A voice near the end of the blue cable car, in North Denver, kept piping: "Right this way; two blocks to the Healer's house." It was not the voice of a professional "barker," but came from a group of young women that sat on the stoop of a pretentious-looking home near the corner of Goss street and Fairview avenue. One of the party explained afterwards that it was a matter of remaining indoors and having the door bell rung by people who wanted to know where the Healer was. "So," said a pert miss, "we just thought we would stay out on the stoop, and when the crowds came by tell them where to find the wonderful man."

The scenes about the Fox residence were the same as on previous days, but in extended form so far as the number of supplicants for relief and curious people, who wanted to see Francis, were concerned. From early in the morning until after the hour when "The New Mexican Messiah" closed his day's work to the public—4 o'clock—the car lines carried thousands to the new mount, and conductors on the lines of cars that go within two blocks of the house said the road never did such a business as was recorded during Schlatter's stay in Denver. All sorts of people tumbled over each other during the earlier hours of the day in their eagerness to be first on the ground. The lame and the halt, the blind, the sufferer from paralysis, and countless others with ailments of various kinds, until the entire list in materia medica would have to be exhausted to name them. It was a strangely odd but fascinating sight.

Francis stood in the yard of the Fox home, his swarthy face illuminated with a glad and peaceful smile and his strong features brought into prominence by the background of his long hair, which fell in ringlets below his shoulders. Outside, extending across the street and up and down the thoroughfare were many hundreds of men, women and children. They seemed to be oblivious to the intensity of the heat, and for hours stood in the sweltering sun, pushing and crowding each other, the sole aim in life being to get close enough to the wonderful man to have him touch them.

All were not ill; many were hale and hearty, but the infection to have Schlatter bless their handkerchiefs or say a word to them was epidemic. In the midst of all the Healer was unperturbed.

He had a kind word for all, and though at times he was closely crowded by the mass of humanity that pressed against the fence that separated them, he managed to attend to the appeals of about 2,000 souls.

An exciting incident occurred about midday, when a large and prosperous looking man who had stood in the sun, succumbed to the effects of the heat and fainted. A pathway was made and Francis made his way to the side of the prostrate man. He took both his hands in his own and almost instantly the stricken man revived and passed out of the crowd with a gladsome smile upon his face. Whether his faint was a ruse in order to save time and get the hand of the Healer was a matter of conjecture, but there were those in the crowd who intimated that such was the plan of the man.

On the outskirts of the crowd were many carriages that contained prominent society buds and matrons. They visited the scene evidently out of curiosity, for they remained in the vehicles, and after watching the strange sight which could only be likened to a Scriptural scene, drove away. As the hour at which the Good Samaritan closed his work approached, the crowd seemed not to have diminished in the least. Intuitively the strange man seemed to know the hour, for just as several watches pointed to the time, he ceased his work, learning first that there were no very urgent cases in the crowd.

His benediction, just prior to retiring indoors, was: "All ye that believe will feel better in three hours. Just believe and thou shalt receive." As Francis pronounced these words he raised his hands, palms down, and bowed his head.

The Healer was found in his study and seated at a desk opening letters, a bundle of something like 150 or 200 being at his right hand. A letter post-marked St. John, from far-away New Brunswick, addressed care of The Daily News, was opened and contained a silk handkerchief, ladies' size, and a request in the letter was that he bless it.

"I receive many such each day," said Francis.

"How do I answer them?" he said, repeating a question. "Oh, that does not bother me; see that pile over there," and Francis pointed to about 100 letters on a side table. "I answered those last evening and did not remain up late either. Yes," he said, "a great many of the letters contained handkerchiefs, but it is not necessary for people to send them. If I write them they will have the same effect, that is, if they have Faith and believe in Him."

Many of the letters, Francis said, simply asked advice and others enumerated ailments for which relief was beseeched. Still others were from people who have experienced the wonderful healing powers of the man and who wrote in grateful words, attesting their Faith in his marvelous powers. One lady, who signed herself Mary Williamson, at Albuquerque, New Mexico, gave permission to publish her letter. In it she expressed thanks for restored health. For over six years Mrs. Williamson suffered from nervous prostration, and in trying to alleviate her suffering became a victim of the morphine habit. She visited Francis while he was at Albuquerque, and testified that the Healer, without know-

MAIL THAT ACCUMULATED UP TO OCTOBER 1ST.

ing her ailment and by simply laying his hands upon her, cured her completely.

Francis was asked why he did not secure the services of a secretary to attend to his constantly increasing correspondence. He shook his head and said it would not do. The work was for him. A letter written by anyone else would have no effect. The Divine power of which he claims to be possessed he said could not be transmitted through others. In this connection Francis said he wished people would write and not come in person. He claimed that he could perform the same miracles through a letter that he could in person, but the people must have Faith.

CHAPTER X.

Zola's materialistic pen could not overdraw the Healer. Five days prior to the close of the work in Denver the union depot was thronged with sick, blind and hopeless, they were guided by Faith in Francis, and they poured through the gates in great crowds. A penitential observance created an air of asceticism that awed the beholders.

In anticipation of the Healer's retreat, which Francis said the Father had marked out for him before his departure for new fields, the mysterious man, who confounded the science of the world was gradually restraining his appetite and partook only most sparingly of the simplest articles of food. One slice of bread and butter and a glass of wine constituted his supper. He ate no meat and intimated that he might fast again. At times there was an air of solemnity about the Healer that filled his faithful attendants with awe. In such moments he had little to say, and the expression on his face indicated that his mind

REAR VIEW OF THE HEALER, TAKEN FROM THE YARD.

was far away. In the opinion of some he was holding communion with a power higher than earth—the power from which he derived the inspiration that carried him through his remarkable exertions from day to day. There was no doubt of a change of some kind in Schlatter. He saw the tremendous responsibility he had undertaken and the procession of pain-stricken and deformed humanity that passed before him each day made a deep impression upon his sympathies.

While he was evidently preparing for greater work than he had ever yet undertaken, he faced the future with absolute Faith in the Divine assistance which he believed accompanied him every moment of his life and directed every action.

"I am nothing," said Francis, as he sat in the room where he made his home for months, "but the Father is everything. Have Faith in the Father and all will be well," was his favorite expression.

Francis returned from the treatment of an invalid, to whom he devoted over two hours. He appeared the image of health, and at the mention of the great crowds which were expected during the last week, his eyes flashed and his face beamed.

"I have treated 1,200 to 1,500 a day up to the present time," said Francis, "but this week they will move faster. There will be some pretty fast work this week."

"Is a quick treatment as efficacious as a long one?" asked a listener.

"Oh, yes," was the reply, "all that is really necessary is for me to touch them, but the people would not be satisfied. In cases where the persons are too weak to stand in line let their friends send a handkerchief. The handkerchief is just as good as a treatment."

"Mr. Schlatter, is it positively sure that you will stop public work soon?"

"That is certain," replied Francis, "I will stop next Friday and go to work upon the letters. I will not attempt to answer any letters, but will return the handkerchiefs. Come and see what I have to do before I get through in Denver."

The Healer led the party to whom his conversation was addressed into a neat little bedroom, where the eye was greeted by a great pile of letters, said to number more than 50,-

000. The letters were piled upon a bed and reached nearly to the ceiling.

"If I should try to answer every one of these," said Francis, "there would be a year's work before me. All I can hope to do is to handle the handkerchiefs and return them by mail."

In speaking of the future, Francis was exceedingly uncommunicative. He said he had set no date for leaving the city and may remain several weeks. His attention was called to the report that friends had leased a hall in which for him to appear after his advent in Chicago.

"They made a mistake," said Francis. "I have not been consulted in the matter, and it is not at all probable that I will go to any hall. I cannot say where I shall stop in the city, how long I will stay or where I shall go when I leave Chicago. The Father will decide."

Schlatter's history showed that if he was not kindly received in any town he obeyed the Scriptural injunction and shook the dust of the place from his feet at the first favorable moment.

His theory was that if one town didn't want him, there were others where he would be welcomed. While the Healer partook of his frugal repast, a long procession passed through the gate at the union depot. Every train that came into the city brought scores of persons who came to Denver for the express purpose of receiving treatment from Schlatter. The Union Pacific train from Omaha brought 250 men, women and children, and the Fort Worth train swelled the arrivals by fifty more. The trains that arrived in the morning and evening carried, in all probability, 600 invalids and their friends. The arrivals announced that the excitement was spreading, and hundreds were expected from single communities during the last week. "Omaha is worked up wonderfully over the cures reported by persons who have come to Denver to meet Schlatter," said a railroad man from the mouth of the Platte river. "I never saw such an excitement as is now in that city. Everybody is talking of the Healer, and people who return after being treated talk for days before the curiosity is satisfied. We know that Schlatter can cure, for he has cured Superintendent Sutherland and many more railroad men. We have been directed to return to Omaha as soon as possible, in order that others may come." When the crowd left Omaha it numbered 150, but accessions were made at North Platte, Grand Island, Sidney, Cheyenne and other stations, which showed that the fever spread all over the Union Pacific system. The movement was the result of an order posted by General Manager E. Dickinson, in which he stated that any employee of the system suffering from physical ailment was at liberty to come to Denver. Passes were issued as fast as called for, and the arrivals stated that this influx was only the advance guard of a much greater army that was to follow as fast as the men could be relieved from duty. There were some pathetic scenes as the great crowds moved through the Union depot. Able-bodied men tenderly carried in their arms the invalids of the family, and tottering steps were supported by strong hands. One case was especially noticeable. The patient was held in the arms of her cousin, a sturdy farmer, who came all the way from Clayton, New Mexico, as attendant upon the woman, who appeared shriveled and bent almost out of human shape from rheumatism. The man carried the woman as

7

though she were a baby, and quickly disappeared in a carriage with his charge. Others were supported on crutches, and many were so weak from the long journey by rail that they were obliged to rest in the depot before proceeding to a lodging place.

"The depot has been a hospital ever since Schlatter began his work in Denver," remarked an observer. "This morning the benches were filled with cripples, and I see a new contingent has put in an appearance. Well, I am not kicking. Schlatter has made nothing out of it, and he has certainly relieved a large amount of pain since he reached this city."

The visitors soon disappeared up Seventeenth street. The great majority sought the cheaper lodging houses and left orders to be called before daylight. The list of arrivals included conductors, engineers, brakemen, shopmen, clerks of department headquarters, and quite a number of section men took advantage of the remarkable notice of the general manager. Many of the employees, to all appearances, were in good health, but it was stated that every person was in some way afflicted, even though it did not present an outward appearance. From the promptness with which many of the strangers started for hotels, it was evident that they learned en route where to find the class of house desired. The Faith of General Manager Dickinson in the Healer was shown by the presence of Mrs. Dickinson in the city. Mrs. Dickinson arrived in a special car early in the morning, and was treated by Francis before 9 o'clock. Owing to the fact that she was almost an invalid, she was given a position near the head of the line and was obliged to wait only a few minutes. It was said that she was afflicted with deafness, and it was largely on this account that she came to Denver. She was accompanied by several lady friends, and left the city immediately after returning to the depot from North Denver. The order of the general manager of the great railway system brought forth general comment when it became known. It was acknowledged that no general manager ever before extended such an opportunity to the employees of a railway. The opinion was that Mr. Dickinson had been profoundly impressed by the cures effected by the Healer.

Railroad men regarded Francis with general favor ever since his advent in Denver, and no class received greater benefit. The railroad companies took in thousands of dollars on account of travel attracted by Schlatter, and lines that extend as far as San Francisco and New York were gainers by the presence of the Healer in Colorado. For some reason Francis was especially accommodating to railway employees, and was at that time giving treatment to several railroad men who were deeply afflicted and could not stand in line. One of the men was blind, and the other was one of the best-known officials in the city. The majority of the railway fraternity were ready to swear by Schlatter, and the number was by no means confined to men of ordinary salaries.

On the 12th of November, 1895, the crowds were immense and showed signs of still increasing. It was a tremendous strain on Francis, apparently, and he treated the crowd at the rate of forty-five a minute. Fully 2,700 people grasped the Healer's hand during that memorable day, while a party of church dignitaries surveyed the crowds. At 11 o'clock in the morning the crowd in front of the residence of Mr. Fox was a sight to behold. It began at the fence in front of the door, where the Healer stood, and stretched to the end of the block,

around the next two sides, and half way down
the fourth side. This was not in a single line,
but four or five abreast. All day long the great
procession moved by the quiet man who had
formed the objective point of their vigil. All
day long he took them by the hand, one after
another, calling down help for their infirmities for each one. It was a procession of the
lame, the halt and the blind, the pale, the feeble and the emaciated, jostling side by side
with the curiosity hunter, and with those apparently in perfect health. The news that
Francis was to depart from his field of labors
in Denver, and that his ministrations here
would soon be over, had spread abroad, and
the crowd of lookers-on, attracted by a desire
to gaze at the man of whom such strange
things were told, was very great. Carriages
drove up at frequent intervals all day, and the
occupants, usually from the wealthier classes,
would sit for a time and gaze over the heads of
the crowd at the Healer's face. No matter
what the opinions of the on-looker might be,
the placid features of Francis seemed to possess a fascination for every visitor. A party
of church dignitaries drove up late in the afternoon in a handsome equipage, drawn by high-

stepping steeds. The representatives of the church gazed at the crowd with a smile which was somewhat patronizing and pitying, but they were, nevertheless, astonished at the size of the crowd. They had not hitherto credited the tales of the numbers who visited the Healer, and had openly expressed doubts as to his having performed any cures whatever. Francis himself looked as fresh as the day he began his herculean labors. He seemed brighter and stronger and more full of power than when he began his work in Denver. Mr. Fox, however, upon whom, next to Francis, the heaviest strain had fallen, looked rather worn. He circulated among the crowd a good deal and examined into individual cases. Late in the afternoon he took a little boy from a carriage and carried him tenderly to the Healer. The child, who had a paralyzed hand and arm, laid his head trustingly upon the shoulder of his protector, and gave his hand confidingly to Francis upon reaching him.

Between 250 and 300 strangers from Kansas and Nebraska were among those treated, and their faces were a study as they gazed at the man of whom they had heard enough to bring them so far. The most salient feature of the day was the number of society people, both in line and present as spectators. The trains that evening brought in hundreds of people, and calls even left at hotel counters for 3 and 4 o'clock in the morning. The Union Pacific train brought in 188 people from Omaha and other points, and Lincoln, Nebraska, sent a party of forty-six in charge of the Burlington representative earlier in the day.

One of the persons who sounded the praises of Francis was Colonel J. K. Keithlay, editor of the "Republican," a paper published at Weeping Water, Nebraska. Colonel Keithlay arrived in Denver and received three treatments for deafness. He carried a rubber tube when he reached Denver, but he now finds no need of the tube, and says he will try to get through the line to-day as a finisher to a remarkable cure. He was at the Oxford hotel.

At the Brown Palace hotel several wealthy men compared notes. Four of them came to Denver to be treated by Francis, and succeeded in buying places in the line at $1.50 in each case. Four men gave up their tickets at the solicitation of the visitors. After they had talked over the experiences of the day, the men came to the conclusion that they had not done the right thing to buy places in the line, when persons suffering more than they and without money were obliged to take their chances of treatment. The four men resolved as a penance to go into line and travel along to the Healer by slow stages, even though it required all day. "It isn't fair," said one of them, "for a man who has plenty of money to purchase any advantage over the distressed-looking and pain-stricken women and children who are to be seen in that line."

The blind conductor, Mr. Ed. Cain, left for McCook, Nebraska, to rest, after having received several treatments from the Healer. His last words at the depot were: "Boys, I expect to see my wife and babies soon. Look out for a telegram." The railroad men awaited returns from the brave-hearted conductor.

CHAPTER XI.

We herewith append a few of the many cases of cures, some of which are authentic and well known, others from a distance. We have had to rely upon others' evidence.

A most notable case is that of Mrs. Stephen Vinot, of this city, who was perfectly helpless, suffering greatly from spasms and other ailments. She had decided to have performed a dangerous surgical operation, when the Healer came to Denver. Instead, she was taken to him and was completely cured. To-day she is one of the Healer's most ardent defenders.

The wife of the Rev. John Turner, 2045 Curtis street, who had been bed-ridden a long time, suffering with paralysis, was cured, and to-day is perfectly well.

One of the most prominent and highly esteemed citizens of Pueblo, Colorado, is Hon. Judge J. W. Kerr, who sounds the praises of Francis Schlatter in the highest key of gratitude and will always appreciate the allevia-

tion afforded him in his distress. Judge Kerr
is a very large man and had been a sufferer
from inflammatory rheumatism. While he
was in the midst of one of these attacks he
visited Denver and called to see the Healer
and received treatment.

To quote the judge's remarks about the disease and the blessing he received from Schlatter would be very interesting, and they are to
this effect, viz.: "I suffered so keenly from
rheumatism that I was often obliged to have
my feet suspended when in my room at the
hotels in order to gain relief. The only relief
seemed to be had in withdrawing the circulation from the extremities as far as possible.
In the fall of each year my sufferings were especially acute, and when the cool weather
came I felt all the old premonitions. Through
a friend of mine in Santa Fe, New Mexico, I
heard of Francis Schlatter and his wonderful
work, who was loud in his praises of the
Healer. When I visited Mr. Fox's house to
see Francis I suffered so much that Mr. Fox
(who is also a friend of mine) took compas-
sion on me and conducted me into his house,
where I met the Healer. The Healer took
hold of my hands and gave me a short treat-

ment. During the treatment I felt no magnetic or electric shock, and as I have looked
into those subjects I believe I know when
such a power is exerted. In fact, I have ex-
perimented in the past and long since discovered that there is a good deal of magnetism about me. I do not attempt to explain the
power of the Healer, but from the minute he
grasped my hands the pain in my feet departed, and after nearly a month I can say that
I have had absolute relief from rheumatic
pains since I met Schlatter. I have been in
the mountains since, have been through vio-
lent snow storms, have been exposed to the
cold and to extreme changes in temperature,
but not a twinge have I felt from rheumatism.
I have a handkerchief which the Healer held
in his hand and I know of no money that can
buy that handkerchief."

Said a young lady: "I was blind. Now I
can tell the color of your eyes. When I can
read a paper I will tell you my name and all
about the blessing this silent man has been to
me."

A majority of those who were treated by
Francis did not give their names or addresses,
but one woman was so joyful over the effects

of the treatment that she proclaimed her happiness. She said that for years she had been
bereft of the use of her arms and limbs, and
that physicians were unable to help her. She
submitted to a treatment by Francis and she
felt splendidly.

William Norris, an engineer on the Atlantic and Pacific railroad, in New Mexico, with
headquarters at Albuquerque, was one of the
many callers on the Healer. He stated that
he was treated by Francis at Albuquerque
several weeks before his arrival in Denver,
and his eyesight, which was failing, was completely restored.

One of the most conspicuous patients was
a poor house patient, who appeared to be in
the last stages of consumption. He had to
be helped into a place in front of the Healer,
and went away electrified.

Another remarkable cure was that of a
stylishly dressed young woman, who wore a
fortune in diamonds on her fingers. She was
wasted with disease, and following the treatment, which consisted of simply laying on of
hands, she wept with joy and needed no assistance in entering a carriage that awaited

herself and her husband. The couple declined to give their names, but they were tourists.

Cured without drugs or charges, was the story related by W. M. Clark, general Eastern freight agent of the Missouri Pacific railroad, in New York City.

Mr. Clark, who had at that time completed a tour of the Western states, saw Francis in Denver, witnessed some of his cures, and, in fact, was cured himself. According to his story, he had a bad cough and, just out of curiosity, passed his handkerchief to the Healer. Francis blessed it and that night Mr. Clark slept with it around his throat, and in the morning his cough had entirely disappeared. Dozens of similar cases were reported to Mr. Clark, who was firmly convinced of the Healer's wonderful healing powers.

One of the division superintendents of the Union Pacific system, Mr. Sutherland, said he was injured in the wreck of his private car over three years ago, and since the time of the accident suffered a great deal. He had four operations performed in the hope of obtaining relief, but to no avail. He attended to his duties, but he could not even move in an office chair without suffering much pain in the back, and it was an impossibility for him to ride in an engine without suffering greatly.

Aside from this, Mr. Sutherland was deaf. After he had returned from Denver he could lift a loaded trunk without pain, and a few days after rode from Valley to Waterloo on an engine without suffering, and his deafness entirely disappeared.

The general manager of the Union Pacific system, Mr. E. Dickinson, posted an order at Omaha, Nebraska, in which he stated that any employee of the system, suffering from physical ailment, was at liberty to come to Denver at the expense of the company. The men were also authorized to bring any and all afflicted members of the family along, and every age and sex was represented in the throng that came.

The daughter of Commissioner P. J. Flynn, of the Western Passenger Association, located in the Union depot, at Denver, Colorado, was cured of diphtheria after a treatment from the Healer.

A Mrs. V. V. Snook suffered greatly from a cancer, and was cured of it and was indeed happy and well in a short time.

A prominent military man of Wyoming took his 12-year-old daughter, who was blind, from birth, in one eye. Colonel Foote was very thankful when the little one looked up into the eyes of her papa and exclaimed: "O, I can see!" The sight was restored instantly.

J. D. Connor, of Omaha, had a little girl who suffered with asthma from birth. He brought his daughter to Denver and returned with her a well and hearty girl. The child had suffered from infancy.

The favorite cook in the private car of the president of the Denver & Rio Grande railroad was afflicted with rheumatism. His fingers were doubled up. They were straightened, and he said he felt thirty-five years younger.

For a long time the right hand of Jim Welsh, of Colorado Springs, was useless. Soon after he was seen shaking hands at the Union depot to show what the Healer had done for him.

Among the cures were several cases of paralysis, one of partial blindness, one of dropsy, and another in which the use of the lower limbs was restored. In one of these cases the cure is attested to by the physician who had been treating the patient, and by others. This was the most remarkable of them all. A lady of Longmont, Colorado, had been suffering with an impaired vision and paralysis of the right arm. She had worn glasses for five years, and her condition was a lamentable one. Dr. D. N. Stradley, of Longmont, treated her, and was assisted by Drs. Callahan and Bickford, also of Longmont. The girl came down to Denver to visit the Healer. She felt better soon after she left here, and when she reached home she could see without the use of her glasses, and could move her arm as if it had never been afflicted. Dr. Stradley, in an issue of the Longmont "Times," testified to the cure of this girl. He said he did not expect to cure her eye trouble, but he did expect to restore her the use of her arm. He concluded that she is now strong and well, her eyesight restored, and her arm free and well. The editor of that paper added his testimony to that of the physician. He said that he knew that her eyesight had been affected and that her arm had been paralyzed, but she is now recovered from these afflictions.

William A. Roach, of Globeville (near Denver), threw away his crutches within thirty minutes after he had seen the Healer. He was thrown from a wagon ten years ago, he explained to a number of people who had gathered around him after the cure was effected, and lost the use of his lower limbs. He walked with difficulty by the use of two crutches, and was assisted by friends to the North Side, where the Healer was. He felt that he was well soon after he left the place, and believes that he is thoroughly cured.

John Doyle, of Boulder, Colorado, said he was carried to the Healer, suffering from paralysis in the left side. His entire side was useless. He was soon able to walk easily and could use both arms. Another surprising cure was that of Mrs. Diana Dill, of Denver. She said she had dropsy in her feet and limbs, and had been treated by three physicians without getting any relief. She was in constant pain, and during the last five months had been unable to wear shoes on account of the swelling. She visited Schlatter, and on the following day the swelling had disappeared, there was no pain, and she was able to put on her shoes.

One of those who were attracted from the Pacific coast by the fame of the Healer was James B. Stetson, a capitalist of San Francisco. Mr. Stetson's sister was badly affected with asthma for many years, and had been try-

8

ing the effects of traveling upon her trouble.
While she was in Boston, Massachusetts, she
read of the remarkable power claimed for the
Healer. In the hope that there might be some
help for his sister, and to leave no possible
source of relief untried, Mr. Stetson brought
her to Denver. She was in one of the carriages
that awaited the pleasure of Francis, while a
tall and fine-looking man, dressed in the latest
style, a wonderful contrast to the man all were
there to see, implored the Healer to see the
sick woman. He was repulsed by some close to
Schlatter, who told him that all were treated
alike, and that the sister must wait. He then
appealed to Mr. Fox. Later the Healer was
seated in that elegant carriage. He took the
hand of the invalid and sat before her for a
time, and looked into her eyes with that
strange look that came into his own at times.
When he left he gave no encouragement. "If
the Father so willed, she will get better; if
not, she must bear her sufferings as best she
can."

Scene Two Blocks Away from the Fox Residence.

CHAPTER XII.

The closing scenes around the Fox homestead, on the afternoon of the 12th of November were ones never to be forgotten.
Bids came in from St. Louis, Mound City,
Omaha, and other cities for the Healer.
It was the old fight between Chicago and
the Missouri city. Citizens of the latter
place made up their minds that Chicago
should not have Francis Schlatter without a
struggle, and their accredited delegate was in
the crowd and authorized to offer Mr. Schlatter
$5,000 if he would come to St. Louis. The gen-
tleman was a well-dressed man, with a busi-
ness-like address, but he was evidently a non-
plussed man when he found that he had struck
a place where money did not talk. He refused
to give his name, for he felt somewhat cha-
grined at the failure of his enterprise, but he
stated that the $5,000 was ready for Mr. Schlat-
ter if he would come to St. Louis, or for any
person who would induce him to go there. He
was very much annoyed at not getting an in-

terview with the Healer, and button-holed Mr.
Fox as soon as he could get through the
crowd, which was not until the Healer had retired for the day. "You might just as well
offer him $5,000,000 as $5,000," said Mr. Fox.
"If he decided to go you wouldn't have to pay
him anything. The very quickest way to keep
him away from your city is to offer him money
for going there." "Well," said the agent, insin-
uatingly, "wouldn't you take the money and
get him to go there?"

"Oh, I couldn't get him to go anywhere,"
said Mr. Fox, drily.

"Well, isn't there anyone in town who would
take the money and influence him to go to St.
Louis?" said the man.

"Guess not, if I couldn't," replied the ex-
alderman, laconically.

"What sort of a man is he, anyway?" queried
the agent explosively, "does he think he's too
good to take money? You can get pretty near
any minister you want for $5,000."

"But Schlatter isn't a minister, you see,"
was the reply, while a humorous twinkle lit
up the North Denver man's eye. "He doesn't
need any money; he has no use for it, and you

càn't bribe him or buy him, and I advise you
not to try it."

The St. Louis man, if that was his home,
went away with a baffled and puzzled expression upon his countenance. It was evidently
something new in his experience. He con-
fessed in his conversation that the scheme was
one of speculation.

When Mr. Schlatter was informed that
there was a man outside who had $5,000 in
his pocket for him if he would go to St. Louis,
he remarked placidly: "I don't want his dollars," and dismissed the subject.

Omaha was also in the field to secure Francis. Omaha, probably more than any other
city, had been stirred up over the tales of the
Healer, and the people were wild there to
have him come.

J. A. Connor, a prominent grain merchant
and an active worker in Y. M. C. A. circles
registered at the Albany yesterday. His mission to Denver was to induce Francis to stop
in Omaha on his way to Chicago. Mr. Connor was acting for a number of the solid men
of Omaha, and he remained in town until he
exhausted every means to induce the Healer
to change his destination. He was accom-

panied by C. K. Spearman, a banker of Gretna, Nebraska, and W. S. Raker, editor of the Gretna Reporter. Five thousand people took Francis by the hand this day. This was the heaviest day's work yet and the crowd was much the largest. Even after he retired to the house they could not be induced to leave, but stood in solid masses, gazing at the house. It was nearly an hour before they finally melted away. After it was over Mr. Schlatter said in conversation that "the power was very strong all day and his neck felt tired."

"Why is that?" was asked him.

"Why," said Francis, "you know the power comes through here,—touching his forehead—"and passes down through my neck."

One of the most remarkable cures of the entire record of the Healer's stay in Denver occurred on this day. The subject was J. P. Handy, of Ellsworth, Kansas. Mr. Handy brought a letter of introduction to E. P. Miller, whose office is in the Opera House block, from Mr. Miller's son, who lives in Kansas and knows Mr. Handy well. Mr. Handy had been a sufferer from rheumatism for a long time, and had been unable to walk without crutches for a long time. He passed through

the line with his wife and received a treatment. Immediately on getting through the crowd that packed the space in front of the Healer he felt his hands relax, as he expressed it, "like a hand opening." He took his crutches from under his arm and walked about without them all the rest of the day. Hundreds saw this and can testify to the instantaneous cure. But few of those, however, who saw him discard his crutches knew that Mr. Handy had several hard lumps or swellings on the palms of his hands. These had been on his hands for many a long day, and Mr. Handy thought they were caused by the excessive pain he had endured. They were gone twenty minutes after he had touched the Healer's hand.

During the last few days of his stay in Denver, detectives were employed to prevent the selling of places in line.

On the morning of the disappearance of the Healer, the bulk of the visitors stood at the spot where they were wont to grasp the man's hand, and not a few put their hands through the fence and held them there a few seconds, as if they could feel the presence of the mysterious power.

At no time did the crowd reach very large proportions, but the people came, as before, by every form of conveyance. Almost all day there were one or two carriages out in the street, and many of the occupants were drawn to the vicinity out of curiosity as well as to get into the presence of the power which was said to linger after the departure of the strange being, through which it was directed toward mankind. Early that morning it became apparent that there was a scarcity of kindling wood in North Denver. The long railing which had been erected to contain the crowds began to disappear, stick by stick. What was left by 10 o'clock Mr. Fox had taken down and placed in his yard, where he devoted it to his own use.

There was a serious side to the disappearance of Francis. Hundreds of people who came to Denver and had not seen the Healer walked the streets as if in hope of his sudden return. They could not convince themselves that their journey was in vain, and did not want to leave for home until every hope of seeing the Healer was gone. Some of the cases were indeed pitiful, but most of them had taken the precaution of sending a handkerchief by mail, and they had that hope to buoy them.

It certainly appeared that the Ruler of the universe sent to this earth the only true apostle in the personage of "The New Mexican Messiah," and who, by his miraculous cures, as the Saviour said, "By my works thou shalt know me." The Healer, by his works, showed the world that he is the true Messiah, who came in obedience to the will of the Father to make the blind to see, the deaf to hear, to heal the infirm and to teach them the word of God. Francis did not receive any of this world's filthy lucre, although it has been offered him, but always refused it, saying: "That it was against the will of his Master."

In New Mexico, at Albuquerque, on more than one occasion, money was forced on him, when he at once distributed it to the poor and needy, retaining nothing for himself. Many of the cures effected through the Healer are certainly not effected by himself but by our Lord and Saviour, Jesus Christ.

The sudden disappearance of the Healer was quite unexpected, but it was the only means he had to get away from the multitude. His whereabouts was a matter of conjecture

and no one knew positively where the Healer
had gone until he was seen passing through
Elizabeth, Colorado, mounted on a white horse.
It was at this point that the missing Messiah
was located early on the morning of the 15th
of November. Francis was riding a fine gray
horse, caparisoned with a brand new saddle.
There was the beard and the wavy hair, which
had become familiar to all who had visited the
Healer and to those who have seen his pictures. In personal apparel, however, the
strange man was much changed. He wore
a bright new woolen hat, brown duck coat,
shoes without heels. Strapped on the horse
was a large pack of bedding. This huge bundle was behind the saddle and was covered
with a new white canvas.

On the afternoon of the evening he left, a
stranger, who gave his name as Scott, appeared in the line and introduced himself to the
Healer. He said he had met the Healer in the
Mojave desert, two years before, and had given
him 50 cents with which to buy food at the
next station. Francis recognized the man and
warmly invited him to call in the evening.
Mr. Scott called, and brought with him a dozen
of his friends. The Healer was somewhat sur-

prised at the number of visitors, but appeared in the best of spirits during the call. The party left before 9 o'clock, with many well wishes for the Healer.

Whether the Scott call had anything to do with his leaving, is not known. Mr. Fox said: "While I do not understand this movement of Schlatter, my Faith in him is not in the slightest degree impaired. I know he was deeply disturbed by the bartering of places in line, and it is possible that he thought of the matter after retiring that night, and left the city in order to avoid the continuance of the practice. The criticism of the preachers and the selling of places in the line were two points upon which Schlatter was especially sensitive. That day the barter all along the line grew to such proportions that it reached his ears several times. He was deeply annoyed, and I feared that he would retire into the house because of the reports that were in circulation as to prices at which the places were sold. He said nothing on the subject during the evening. He was so busily engaged until he retired for the night that there was little opportunity for him to talk. So far as I can see, there was no other reason for him to leave Denver."

One of the rumors that gained some credence was that Francis was to be arrested.
Such was not the case, and I herewith append
an interview from the "News" in relation to it:

"Francis Schlatter was not wanted by the
federal authorities, and they did not issue any
attachment from the United States court.
They made no attempts to ascertain the whereabouts of the Healer. Technically, the missing man might be held for contempt of court
in not appearing as a witness in the case then
pending before United States Commissioner
Capron. Francis was not involved in any way
in the outcome, as he was not made defend-
ant. He was wanted as a witness on the point
as to whether he really 'blessed' the handkerchiefs which defendants are charged by Postoffice Inspector McMechen with using the
mails to fraudulently dispose of. The return
of United States Marshal Israel, on file in the
district attorney's office, showed that Francis
was served with the subpoena to appear on
Thursday morning (the morning of his disappearance). The writ was read to him, but it
did not appear that any copy of the same was
left with him. The probability was, that as
the marshal simply told him of the contents

of the paper, that Francis paid little attention
to the matter, and the fact that he was wanted
in the commissioner's court on the day he disappeared may have escaped the Healer's mem-
ory altogether. No formal application was
made for an attachment for Francis, and if it
were Judge Hallett would not have granted it.
When he was spoken to on the subject by court
officials, the judge remarked: 'I do not think it
is a case where an attachment should issue.'

" 'We do not care particularly as to whether
Schlatter is found or not,' said United States
District Attorney Johnson. 'If he had been
sworn he would have testified that he did not
"bless" the handkerchiefs in question. There
is nothing strange about the method of his disappearance. He is the kind of a man who
would be far more apt to leave on foot in the
night time than go on the cars, if the opportunity were offered him to go by the usual
traveled route. The government will not attempt to locate him.' In the talk which the
district attorney had with Francis, the Healer
told him his position in relation to Faith. 'If
men wish to believe in creation rather than the
Creator,' said Francis, 'the Father lets them go
that way. But if they will have Faith in the

Creator Himself, He will cure all their ills.' Francis said that the Father did it all, and that people should not thank him for cures effected. The case in which Francis was wanted as a witness was adjourned until the following morning, with the idea that the government would secure his attendance by bench warrant. As this course was not pursued, the prosecution was dismissed and defendants were discharged."

The only message he left was the following:

"Mr. Fox—My mission is finished. Father takes me away. Good-bye.

　　　　　"FRANCIS SCHLATTER.

　"November 13."

And thus ended in Denver the mission of a man whom, to all outward appearances, was of God.

FRANCIS SCHLATTER.

Beautiful spirit, sent down to our earth
To gladden the hearts of some by thy birth;
Let thy light shine in splendor and glory,
Christ-like and grand, as is writ in the story.

Beautiful angel from the spiritual world,
Out to the millions thy banner unfurled,
Attracting their souls from death and from
      sin,
To crucified Jesus, our Lover and King.

Go forth to the homeless, by poverty stricken,
Untaught in the love that leads to the heaven.
Save them from sickness and sorrows untold,
Enlist them as soldiers of Christ's beautiful
      fold.

God bless thy mission, thy powers increase
In works of healing, never to cease.
To the lowly and ignorant hold forth thy light,
Guide them safely through life's perilous night.

Sin, sorrow and selfishness soon will decay—
We hail thee as beacon light of a new day,
When millions of souls will arise in their might
And enlist for the teachings of Christ and the
      right.

CHAPTER VIII.

"Modern Miracles" was the subject chosen by Rev. Myron W. Reed for his sermon in the Broadway theater one Sunday morning. A great audience was present, and the gifted speaker proved fully equal to the occasion. Mr. Reed declared warmly in favor of the New Mexican Messiah. He chose his text from Isaiah xi., 28: "Hast thou not known? Hast thou not heard that the everlasting God, the Lord, the Creator of the ends of the earth, fainteth not, neither is weary? There is no searching of His understanding."

He said:

"Mr. Hume, in his famous essay, says that miracles are contrary to experience, and so disposes of miracles. It is easy to grant that they are contrary to the experience of Mr. Hume, probably contrary to the experience of his neighbors. But it is possible to believe that things have happened outside the experience of Mr. Hume, outside the experience of Mr. Hume's neighbors. As a boy I saw the planting of telegraph poles and the stringing of the wire. The old keeper of the village tavern and I listened to the singing of the wire in the wind. In a low, awe-struck voice, he explained the sound to me. 'My son, do you hear that? They are transveying news.'

"If by the word 'miracle' a man means something in violation of the laws of the universe, or something that interferes with them, then I say 'miracles do not happen.'

"It is possible that we are not altogether acquainted with the laws of the universe. Something may happen according to law outside our knowledge. It is old, but interesting to remember that the first ship driven by steam that crossed the Atlantic had on board an able essay proving that it could not be done. It is only a little while ago that an electric car did not seem to be electric. The passenger held on to his nickel to save it if the thing balked.

NOT A MATERIAL THING.

"A mother in Ireland cables a message to her daughter in New York. Under the ocean that message has no body; it is no more a material thing than a flash of lightning. It

9

crosses. The Atlantic cannot wreck it; it ar-
rives. It is possible and probable that the message can cross without the wire. Friends are
able to shoot their thoughts from one to the
other; all that is necessary to perfect the ability is practice. Although up to date, I have
more confidence in the Western Union.

"Every year of the last fifty years has
brought something to light not contrary to experience, to outside experience.

"But miracles are an old fashion. I picked
up the life and works of Elijah and Elisha
last night and re-read the story. It is not wonderful that men of that kind should do works
of that kind. Their works are in the same
great style as themselves. It is not wonderful
that Shakespeare has written Hamlet. Given
Shakespeare, the play of Hamlet is what you
expect of him. Elijah comes out of the canons
of Gilead. Of his birth and childhood we know
nothing. When we first see him he is a man
dressed in a rawhide kilt and a sheepskin mantle, and he proceeds at once to make himself
disagreeable to a king and queen and the ecclesiastical machine of the time. He did some
notable miracles, called down fire from heaven, fire that burned water. He was an un-

equal man. One day he was more than enough
for several hundred priests of Baal, and one
day he was in mortal fear of one woman, flung
himself under a juniper tree and wished that
he were even dead. God was good to him,
put him to sleep and fed him. And in the
strength of the reinforcement of that sleep and
that breakfast, he marched forty days to Ho-
reb, the mount of God. Reading the lines of
the miracle workers as written in the Bible, I
find that they did not hold their gift in absolute continuing possession. It was not their
property. They could not do anything of themselves. The minute they depended upon themselves they broke down.

WAS DONE "IN HIS NAME."

"Whatever good and great thing they did,
they did it in the name of God. 'In His name'
seems to be the faithful formula of the apostles. They make sorry work of it when they
attempt anything alone. St. Paul could heal
the sick sometimes. Even handkerchiefs that
he had touched carried health in them sometimes. But we read that he left his friend and

comrade, Timothy, sick at a certain place. If
he could have cured him doubtless he would.
For some good reason sickness was good for
Timothy. He was to work among people, sick
people, sinful and sorry people. One who has
never been sick makes a wretched nurse. He
will sit down by the bedside of the sufferer
and read a newspaper and chew gum and slide
down into a healthy slumber, like a well infant. Curing others, St. Paul could not cure
himself. He was subject to some kind of physical torment, probably some trouble with his
eyes. All the old prophets and saints were
made to know that they were absolutely de-
pendent on God. Whenever they became self-
conceited and self-sufficient they went to pieces
like Peter on the sea, like Peter on the porch.

"Elijah, about to die, saw Elisha plowing and
went to him and cast his sheepskin mantle over
him and left him to carry on his work. We
know little or nothing of the childhood of
Elisha. He came when he was called. He
did not have to be spoken to but once. He had
intuition, he was a natural man, unspoiled by
civilization. He did miracles. A boy, the son
of his friend, was sunstruck in the harvest
field. She sent for the prophet and he came,

but the boy was dead, but he went into the
room, shut the door and stretched himself
upon the child, mouth to mouth, eyes to eyes,
hands to hands, and the child grew warm and
the child opened his eyes. Before Elisha did
this 'he prayed unto the Lord.' Here is complete self-surrender.

WHY NOT RAISE ALL THE DEAD?

"But some men will say, why not raise all
the dead? It is not expedient. I should think
twice and a long time both times before I
would call any one back who has gone away.
I believe death is a promotion, an incident of
life.

"The chief of the apostles says, 'death is
gain.' For a sufficient reason our Lord called
Lazarus back from the other side of death.
There was a public reason for it. But personally, for Lazarus, it was a coming back to
be questioned concerning things he had no
words for. The men who hated Jesus hated
him; they went about to kill him. It was a
coming back to dust and weariness, to Hamlet's 'sea of trouble.'

"The miracles of the Bible were not wrought as shows, simply to excite wonder and please a mob of the curious. There is sufficient reason for them. Some of them are in answer to Faith that Faith may be encouraged. Some are in answer to little Faith that little Faith may grow. Some are wrought where there is no Faith that Faith may come. All suffering and loss and failure are to lead men to God. We are led and we are driven. We are met more than half way. One way or another we are going to be made to think. I was always half sorry for the issue at Waterloo, but I have no doubt that personally, St. Helena was good for Napoleon. No more campaigns to plan, no more battles to fight, no noise but the noise of the sea. Flags and drums and the voices of cannon are a powerful diversion. Failure along a mistaken road is a good thing. Men must be made to think. I have not much confidence in sermons, but I have in the events of life.

"There is no God, the foolish saith,
    But none there is no sorrow;
And nature oft the cry of Faith
    In bitter need will borrow.

"Eyes that the preacher could not school
  By wayside graves are raised,
And lips say, God be pitiful
  That ne'er said, God be praised.

"When it comes to me I see no use in pain,
when it comes to other people I see uses for it.

"Not all Syria was made healthy in the days
of Jesus Christ. In one place he could not do
mighty works because of unbelief. The people would not let Him in.

"The world is divided into two kinds of people, those who do something and those who
sit on the fence and wonder why they don't
do it the other way. There are vastly more
critics than authors. Naaman, the Syrian,
had leprosy of the old white kind, and the
prophet told him to wash in the Jordan seven
times, and he thought of the bigger rivers
nearer by, and by the side of which Jordan
was an insignificant creek, and went away in
a rage. But his kind of leprosy was fatal, and
death was near and he did as he was told, 'and
his flesh came again like unto the flesh of a
little child, and he was clean.'

"No prophet has told him to do it, but I
understand that the president of 'the light of

the world company' is going to bathe in the Jordan. All the prophets have told him to do something else.

BEST BREASTWORK.

"After all our work on forts with walls of stone and iron, after all our Gibraltars and Quebecs, there is no breastwork against bullet and ball and shell so effective as a bank of plain simple earth. There is a singular power in simplicity. 'Eloquence,' says Mr. Ingersoll, 'is not up among the stars, it is down in the grass.' The old prophets dressed roughly. Low living and high thinking have commonly gone together. We shall remember Robert Burns several days after we have forgotten Chauncey Depew.

"There was a man sent from God whose name was John. He dressed roughly as Elijah, he lived on locusts and wild honey and came out of the wilderness. And some said he had a devil. You remember the various names that greeted Jesus. It may be doubted that a man has lived a true, brave life unless he has been in jail. The jail in history has had the same transformation in degree as the

cross. A man in jail in Woodstock, Illinois,
for the past few months has been in first-rate
company. There is good company in there yet.

"The Bible is a book of expectation; there
is a movement in it. However sorrowfully it
begins it ends with a song. All creation finally
sings. It is a book of hope. Finally 'hard times
come again no more.' The promises of God do
not taper off and become more and peaked
as the centuries go by. They broaden. There
is an increasing purpose. 'The thoughts of
men are widened in the process of the song.'
'Hast thou not heard that the everlasting God
fainteth not, neither is weary?'

"We may not climb the heavenly steps
    To bring the Lord Christ down;
In vain we search the lowest depths,
    For Him no depths can drown.
"No fable old, nor mythic lore,
    Nor dream of bards and seers,
No dead fact stranded on the shore
    Of the oblivious years.
"But warm, sweet, tender, even yet
    A present help is He;
And Faith has still its Olivet
    And Love its Galilee.

"That is Whittier. Isaiah and Whittier agree that God is not getting feeble. The book of Isaiah is full of visions of what is to come. So is the book of Tennyson. All are to know the Lord. Many have postponed these fulfillments to a place called Heaven. There is no reason why that I know of. There is nothing the matter with the sunrise or sunset. I am satisfied with the mountains and I am satisfied with the sea. The earth is a good enough stage for the plays of Isaiah and even of St. John.

"I expect much from these closing years of this century. The last years of the eighteenth were eventful. An anonymous friend asked me to read the first chapter of Charles Dickens' 'Tale of Two Cities.' The times now are as full of signs as the times were full of signs then. Here is a picture of the period before the revelation that, as Thomas Carlyle says, 'let kings know that there was a joint in their necks:'

" 'It was the best of times, it was the worst times, it was the age of wisdom, it was the age of foolishness, it was the epoch of belief, it was the epoch of incredulity, it was the season of light, it was the season of darkness, it was the spring of hope, it was the winter of despair, we had everything before us, we had nothing before us, we were all going direct to heaven, we were all going direct the other way. In England and France it was clearer than crystal to the lords of the state preserves of loaves and fishes that things in general were settled for ever.

"'It was the year of our Lord, 1775. Spiritual revelations were conceded to England at that favored period. Daring burglaries by armed men and highway robberies took place in London every night.' There is much more of it, and all thoughtful writing.

"These days are as those days. We are told that the harvest is abundant, that the hero of Homestead has raised wages, that Atkinson has invented a workingman's salvation stove. We hear also of hunger and now and then of starvation and often suicide. I am not going into statistics of prosperity and of misery. It is the best of times and it is the worst of times. Things are getting ready for a change by and by, and soon the people will have suffered enough. They at last are beginning to think and soon they will begin to do. We are not going back to kings, we are going on to equal freedom, equality of opportunity, special privileges to none.

"Men are rapidly coming to themselves. We have seen what man has done with material things in the last sixty years. We are now to see what he can do with mental things, with, if you please, spiritual things. Man is being revealed to himself. He has been working on things outside himself, on wood and steel and steam and lightning. He is now turning his attention to the undiscovered powers and faculties and privileges of his own soul. I remember Olney's atlas. I studied it forty years ago. Vast regions were marked 'unknown.' They are known now. In the map of a man much is marked 'unknown.' The best in us is weak and almost dead for lack of exercise. It is just beginning to dawn on a good many of us that to get on in life, to make money, or position, or power of a vulgar sort, that this is not the chief end of living. We begin to see that there is something real and substantial and eternal in the life of Jesus Christ. There has never been a time in the history of the race when so many people were dissatisfied with the things that are seen. There are many meetings of more than two or three met

SCENE AT MID DAY, OVER THE BRIDGE.

together reverently to explain the unknown
country of the mind and of the spirit. We are
in earnest to find out what we are and what
we can do.

SCHLATTER'S PATH NOT EASY.

"I have been much interested the past week
in the spectacle over the bridge—in the people gathered together to take the hand of a
man who seemed to be absolutely willing to
be used as God pleases. He will not be paid
and will not be thanked. He says, 'Thank the
Father.' I have read of Joan of Arc. A girl
of 19, a peasant, educated to spin and take
care of sheep. Walking in the garden she
heard 'beautiful voices.' You know her great
story. Until her work was finished always
she heard the beautiful voices in 'Child of
God, go on, go on!' and she obeyed. I have
listened to this man. It does not appear that
he chose this work; it appears that he was
chosen for it. Long he argued with himself
for and against strict obedience to the voice
he heard. It has not been an easy path he
has trod from Denver to the Pacific and back
again, depending always on what is to him the

voice of the Father. This man has walked
across deserts and over mountains, slept in
rain and sleet and snow, asked for food when
told to ask for it, gone without when told to
go without. I talked with a locomotive engineer who on his trips often passed him. He
said: 'If I could have found him at a station
I would have taken him aboard and paid his
fare. But as it happened, I always saw him
between stations.' But you here have read
the main incidents of the later life of this
man. I do not wonder that people go to get
help from him. I believe that he has observed
the conditions of power. He has taken no
care of himself. He has gone where he believes he was sent. He has done what he believes he was told to do. He is the only man
of the kind and degree that I ever saw. If
the people cannot get good from God through
him I do not know why. He has conformed.
It is the most literal following of Jesus Christ
that I have ever known. It was to be expected
that he would be treated harshly. Some people have fully met the expectation. A dis-
tinguished clergyman of this city, who is apt
to say bright things, is reported to have said
that the reason that the clergy did not in-

In Line for Treatment.

dorse the man was because if they did the people would expect them to do what he is doing, and they don't know how.

"This man has made me ashamed of my easy way of taking hold of my work. He has helped me morally. The day after I met him I took hold of a disagreeable, painstaking job that but for the interview I should certainly have declined. I have a strong dislike to the disagreeable. He has cured me of that.

"I shall present no statistics as to cures accomplished. That is not my point to-day. The point is this: We read the Bible; we read there of the sick cured by men who were obedient to God as they understood Him; we read of conditions of power not limited to any country or years. Let any man, any time or anywhere, conform to the hard, self-denying, painful conditions, and God, through him, will do His work. As I have suggested, there may be many who will be compelled to suffer a while longer. As our mild visitor says, 'They will suffer until they think it will be as the Father pleases.' He is doing good here; he is calling our attention to the fact that the center and source of all life is God; not a God who a long time ago filled a cistern and then went away, but God, a free-flowing spring, a 'present help in every time of need'—Immanuel! 'God with us.'

HE IS DOING GOOD.

"He is doing good, as he is lifting our minds and our eyes from the earth. There is a larger thing than real estate. I have been over this scene often. I see there the people who need help, old and young, all sorts and conditions, women with babies, and this comes to me— the scene suggests the lines:

" 'The Master has come over Jordan,
  Said Hannah, the mother, one day;
He is healing the people that throng Him
  With a touch of His finger, they say.
So now I shall carry the children—
  Little Rachel and Samuel and John,
And dear little Esther, the baby,
  For the Master to look upon.'

"Once in our lives we have an opportunity to see a man who does not take care of himself. He has lost himself in his work.

"I look at this pathetic figure emerged from the desert, and I mentally contrast him with some soft soldier of the cross who reads a sermonette and then says: 'I am prostrated.' He

CRIPPLED LADY JUST AFTER TREATMENT.

don't say tired; that wouldn't use up the alphabet fast enough. 'Take up your cross and follow Me,' says the Master. Many a time I have dodged that commandment.

"This man will help us to be brave."

The following is an open letter, written in reply to a criticism of the Rev. G. L. Morrill, pastor of Calvary Baptist Church, Denver:

To the Rev. G. L. Morrill:

The coming of Mr. Schlatter has turned the thoughts of many into the paths of a religious investigation who otherwise would have continued to rest in material thoughts, and this is true notwithstanding your declaration that his coming has caused Christ to be caricatured, the Bible belittled, the spirit slighted, infidelity increased and religion retarded. This thought will continue and bear its good fruit, notwithstanding oratorical frothings of certain orthodox ministers.

Mr. Schlatter's advent was without show or display, peaceable and quiet, "with malice toward none and charity for all," yet you find fault that he, smarting under the cruel thrusts of the orthodox pulpit, uttered a mild rebuke against those who barter and trade in the sanctuary of the Lord and claim a mortgage upon

10

the soul of man "from the cradle to the grave"
for the advancement of their particular creed
or dogma. Do you forget that, in far more sav-
age terms, Christ rebuked the wealthy ministers of the Pharisee church of his day, and the
man who "beholdest the mote in his brother's
eye, but considerest not the beam in his own
eye?"

Your attack on Mr. Schlatter seems to my
mind more in the nature of an attack on his
claim that a life of devotion to God and His
work and earnest prayer has brought to him a
spiritual power. And in meeting his claim you
rest satisfied in the utterance of a few cheap
jokes and flippant conclusions, more fitted to
a political rostrum than the sacred precincts
of the sanctuary, and a few choice epithets,
such as "imposter," "insane," "ignorant,"
"blasphemer," etc., etc., as a fitting conclusion
to your discourse. These are the weapons of a
weak cause.

Jesus was looked upon by the world as an
imposter, and was adjudged guilty of blas-
phemy by the church of those times, and crucified. John the Baptist was adjudged a bab-
bling lunatic, cast into prison and beheaded
in order to stop his alleged insane utterances.

You call Mr. Schlatter ignorant and say he has no inclination to read and study, and thus ignores the scriptures, for it is written, "that man be without knowledge is not good." If you mean he is without worldly knowledge, he has his excuse for such deficiency in the scriptures, for it is said, "For the wisdom of this world is foolishness with God, for it is written, He taketh the wise in their own craftiness." And can you point to any portion of the teachings where it is held the duty of man to seek worldly wisdom? Does not the whole secret doctrine go to establish the fact that "to know God and keep His law is the whole duty of man?" Were the twelve taken from the experts in worldly wisdom or from the fisherman's net?

Again, you say: "Mr. Schlatter a few years since denied and disavowed God, but now professes to heal the sick in His name." Is it possible you have also forgotten the character of Paul on the way to Tarsus, the chief of sinners and blasphemers, as Paul himself testifies, bent upon destroying the followers of his Christ? And do you not know that if the gospel was deprived of the interpretation of his

inspired pen, that there would be far more excuse for our groping about in darkness in
search of "the straight and narrow path?"
And did not Jesus and Peter and James and
Paul silently steal away in the night time when
the persecution of their enemies retarded their
work, and have you not spoken of their flight
in burning words of pathos from the same pulpit from which you denounce a lowly follower
of the Nazarene, and advocate that the "hounds
of the law" be put on his tracks, that he may
be brought back and whipped of human justice?

However, my brother, the personality of Mr.
Schlatter in the controversy his presence has
engendered is of small importance, and is of
little moment to you and me, and you mistake
the question if you think so. The question is,
Shall they who believe on Christ and understand His law and keep it receive the spiritual
power promised in St. John iv., 12, or is this
promise a hollow mockery, and is a soul of
gentleness, goodness, Faith, meekness, tem-
perance and brotherly love, subordinate to and
at the mercy of the "flesh," the errors of the
human mind, which Christ said "is a liar from
the beginning and the father of it?"

You occupy the exalted position of spiritual adviser to a portion of the community. We have a right to expect those in your calling to point out with unerring finger the "straight and narrow way." Yea, more; we have a right to demand that all such shall remove themselves from human prejudice, bias, passion, dogmas and man-made creeds, and, placing the heel of truth upon the material serpent, rise into the pure realm of spirit as far as the imprisoned soul may, and then answer the inquiries of the wayfaring brother in the spirit of truth and understanding. In the same spirit, as a seeker after the true light and understanding of the gospel, I ask you to explain the following passages of scripture:

After Jesus had risen from the tomb He said: "And these signs shall follow them that believe. In my name shall they cast out devils; they shall speak with new tongues; they shall take up serpents; and if they drink any deadly thing it shall not hurt them; they shall lay hands on the sick and they shall recover." Also: "I say unto you, he that believeth on Me, the works that I do shall he do also; and greater works than these shall he do, because I go unto the Father." Also: "Wherefore I say unto you, what things soever ye desire, when ye pray believe that ye receive them and ye shall have them." Are these promises made by Christ null and void in our generation? Have they been released by a later edict of God? If so, when and where? If they are not efficacious in our day, why have they a place in our gospel? And here is another: "And His disciples asked Him why they could not cast out the deaf and dumb spirit, and He said unto them: 'This can come forth by nothing but by prayer and fasting.'" Was Jesus also mistaken in regard to prayer and fasting?

It has been said this power was given only to the twelve and the seventy disciples. This answer will not do. There is no authority in the scriptures for such claim. It must be untrue, for His followers healed all manner of sickness for three centuries after His crucifixion. And there is no evidence in the gospel that God was guilty of class legislation. His promises were for all mankind for all time and place, and there is no statute of limitation running against them.

One more question: Is it not a fact that sickness is the second stage of sin, and death the third, and that they are all the result of diso-

bedience of the spiritual law, and that Christ
recognized no so-called material law as holding
the issues of life and death? And do not the
first six verses of Matthew ix. unequivocally
establish that sin and sickness are synono-
mous, and the healing of the sick was the de-
struction of sin? Is not the casting out of evil
spirits or material thoughts the spiritual pan-
acea for all sin and sickness and the power
through which death is overcome?

I ask these questions in the spirit of earnestness. I am a wanderer in the wilderness between sense and soul. I may have crossed the
"narrow way" many times, but in my blindness
have not seen it. Let the light of your understanding shed its beams, and possibly others
may discover the way into the "land of promise."*

N. B. BACHTELL.

*Illustrations by permission, W. A. White, Artist.

CHAPTER XIV.

———

"The understanding is the vestibule of the mind! Uncover thy head and enter the temple of the soul! Behold the power, the beauty and the love! If we had nothing but understanding, how little should we know or think or feel!"—Horatio Stebbins.

THE POWER OF THE MAN.

The leaving of Francis Schlatter from Denver closed one of the most remarkable and sublime manifestations of the power of God this century has ever witnessed. Throughout his whole mission in Denver he demonstrated the power for good, physically and spiritually, that was unsurpassed or even equaled by any human manifestation since the days of the apostles. That the man was endowed with Divine power, hundreds of the people firmly believed. His fast of forty days in New Mexico (of which to me there was no doubt) demonstrated that some hidden

The Only Rainy Day in Fifty-Eight.

power more potent than mere physical or human must have sustained him. Another demonstration which was truly wonderful was at the end of that great event, eating a hearty meal in his depleted condition. All the authorities at the time said he would surely die, yet, he not only lived, but in six days thereafter he made a trip of 600 miles to Denver, that is really fatiguing to an ordinary person in good health and able to stand the long, tedious journey. Upon his arrival in Denver he was very thin in flesh, not weighing to exceed 100 pounds. Again that inscrutable power asserted itself, and in ten days his condition was normal and he stood forth a perfect man. During all the time he was recuperating he daily answered all the mail that came to him, which was quite large, and also treated a great many people, so that he virtually had had no rest. When on the morning of September 16 he began public treatment, this remarkable endurance of the man, when for fifty-eight days he pressed the hands of thousands of people, was another great manifestation of this great power. His life, while in Denver, was of the simplest.

Kind and loving; happy when he could help

some poor suffering soul. In the family circle
at Mr. Fox's, when his work of healing was
done for the day, he was like a child and
would smile at the ludicrous incidents of the
day as they were related to him. In addition
to treating in public, he frequently would go
nights to people who were unable to leave
their beds. Among some of the numerous
cases may be mentioned that of Mrs. George
Waterbury, at whose house he treated her
little boy for two weeks. Mrs. Waterbury's
little child, George, met with an accident
when only seven days old, through the care-
lessness of the nurse, who let the little infant fall from out her arms, sustaining par-
alytic stroke, the result of a contusion of the
spine. The little boy was also speechless, having no control over the vocal chords. For
three days at a time he would lay in spasms,
and the mother thought there was no relief
for her child but death. In appearance this
baby is fat and very healthy looking, is very
bright and understands a great deal, though
unable to speak intelligently as yet. The
child could not utter a sound beyond a cry
before Francis treated the little one, and now
he is able to speak his sister's name, Min (Min-

LITTLE HARRY WEBBER IN FRONT OF CARRIAGE.

nie), and A for that of Ada. When the Healer
would take his tiny hands and treat him, he
would look up into his face most pitifully,
and exert the muscles in his throat in an attempt to speak. The Healer spent Sundays
here and enjoyed his visits. Mr. Waterbury,
who is a postoffice inspector of this division,
met Francis while in New Mexico and gave
him a letter of introduction to his wife. When
he arrived in Denver, Francis presented the
letter to Mrs. Waterbury, whereupon she
accepted the letter but did not read it, saying, "I need no introduction." This evidently
pleased Francis, as it was her Faith that
helped to bring the child where it is to-day.
The writer called at the above residence, in-
terviewed the lady and saw the child.

A very interesting case was that of Mrs.
Richard Webber's son, Henry, who was an
invalid with that dreaded affliction—hip disease. This family were the first people in
Denver to call on the Healer. Henry suffered over three years, and was in plaster
Paris three times and iron braces twice; was
unable to go to bed. About a week before
the Healer arrived his mother had to undress
him and then remain up all night long for

nights, and was almost disheartened. His cure was gradual, though effective, and from the time he was treated he never once said, "Mamma, I feel so tired." His left limb had shrunken over three inches and now it is almost the normal length and he goes about without the use of his crutches.

The accompanying picture shows little Henry on crutches in the crowd. The morning the author called he had been climbing trees. He has never taken a spoonful of medicine since the day he was treated. When Francis left Denver, Henry sobbed bitterly, as though he had lost his best friend.

The Healer called many times to treat Mrs. Harry L. Sedley, and I quote her letter, which she has written to me under date of October 1, 1896:

"I had been an invalid for two years, and had given up all hope of ever having my health restored. I first heard of the Healer through the newspapers, and I thought if I could only live until he came to Denver I could be cured. Through the kindness of Mrs. George Waterbury, he came to my house to see me. The evening he came I had been given up by two of the best doctors in Denver, and all my friends were just waiting for me to die. He took hold of my hands and gave me a treatment, and told me the Lord was not ready for me yet, that I would get better, but it would take a long time. He also blessed a handkerchief for me, which I have continued to wear. I began to improve right away, but have been quite sick since, and had doctors. Both claimed the only way to be cured was by an operation. But I still had Faith in the Healer and continued wearing the handkerchief, and now I am able to go all over the city and am about cured. I have no hesitancy in saying it was the Healer and my Faith in him and God that brought me out of my serious sickness."

Throughout all his ministry he would not and did not receive a cent for his work in any way or manner, nor would he accept it. In some instances the people would ask what was the price. His answer would be, "Have Faith; that is the only price I charge."

FAITH.

"We chitchat; we character events; we plan and purpose human action, while we ourselves are blind to truth."

To guard against all evil, whether it is caused consciously or otherwise, is to attain force of character; to make it plainer, Faith in the omnipresent source of all power within this earthly tabernacle, man's soul. "Without Faith ye are nothing," remarked the Saviour. This means the will must not be clouded with doubt. "Fear and doubt are the hell-born daughters of ignorance, that drag men down to perdition; while Faith is the white-robed angel that lends him her wings and endows him with power."

When we become thoroughly conscious of that inner life and realize its true meaning, then, and not until then, can we hope to attain unto that perfection to which we are all entitled by Divine inheritance. Faith is the ladder we must climb, and as we go through life many reverses will occur and disappointments may come; yet, after all, they are blessings in disguise, though at the time they occurred it was so hard to endure them!

Penetrating through the windows of the soul and searching within ourselves, we find what most people term the intuition—that special power through which we realize we are united to the Omnipotent, the original fountain of all life. And we are always in positive touch with this unlimited fountain head, because we are told in the scriptures, "In God we live, move and have our being." Many of us are not aware of the close union. The immediate perception in the human race is that by which he or she is vigilant of or perceives the holy presence in such a plain manner that the person receives impressions through it which will guide his or her life into lofty channels of utility and gracefulness, if it is heeded cautiously and improved by yielding to their direction.

This faculty in man and woman corresponds to the instinct of the lower animals, but there is a vast difference between the two. The intuition of the human race is conscious, while that of the dumb animal is not conscious. In one sense of the word these two faculties are allied, but they are distinct steps of gradual unfoldment. Intuition or instinct (in reality they are one) is the intermediate space of the Creator and the created. In the human being it befits the conscious joining with itself and God, the workshop by which God becomes the good that may be seen.

The revealing of this faculty furnishes us with life-giving, musical truth around ourselves, so that we can come in contact with and conquer all impediments in our pathway of life. Through this gateway we come into conscious atonement with the God-power, unbounded knowledge and everywhere present good. The question naturally arises, is Faith allied to this faculty, or is it entirely different and distinct from it? The bursting forth of a ray of light disperses the darkness; so likewise the intuition, more or less splendor, according as this faculty is unfolded in the person, the effulgence of his glory, guiding toward a higher place, and aiming to glittering distances in advance that may be gained, through that endeavor which reclines on a safe credence in the everywhere present God. This diffusing stream of light is Faith, and it is a pure streamlet that has its source in that faculty called the "Intuition."

These sacred communications of the intuition are bits of truth that crumble off by coming in touch with the one great mind, "as

Job walked and talked with God" in the days
of the prophets, and may be tried by those
who unfold their intuition, and the splendor
and clearness of these trials will rest entirely
upon the development. The higher the unfoldment, the clearer the perceivement of
truth and the less the deviation from truth.
Faith in this exhaustless stream is what humanity needs, and when these impressions
come, trust them, and you may rest assured
you will go through life in the right direction.
This faculty is so dormant in some people that
it does not disclose any realized truths; nevertheless, with care and proper nourishment
(good thoughts) it guides and governs the rest
of the faculties. Believe, wait and trust for
the still, small voice within your earthly tabernacle and you will soon detect its voice.
When we lose ourselves in the Omnipotent,
this faculty will divulge with so much force
that the whole life will be instituted on the
"Petrous" of everlasting truth, and erring
from the pathway of duty will be less frequent.

Oh, for more Faith, bright, clear Faith in
the Divine power of God to heal the body and
save the soul. He is the same to-day as He

11

was eighteen hundred years ago, when the centurion besought Him, saying his servant was sick of the palsy, and Jesus said, "I will come and heal him." The centurion replied, "Lord, I am not worthy thou shouldst come under my roof. Say but the word and my servant shall be healed."

What perfect Faith! He believed that Jesus had power to heal and the Saviour was willing to honor his Faith, when he said, "Thy Faith hath made thee whole. Go! thy servant is healed."

It is also the same faith manifested by Abraham in offering up his only son. He believed God, and it was imputed to him for righteousness. It is Faith like this we must have in the promise and power of God. Take him at his word. As our Faith is, so be it unto us, simple and childlike in power of God. This Faith was what Francis Schlatter possessed. He, in his sweet, childlike way, asked the Father and received.

CHAPTER XV.

Rev. Edward Southworth, at Booth school house, spoke on "In the Messianic Shadow," having reference to the work of Francis Schlatter. He selected his text from Acts v., 15: "They brought forth the sick into the streets and laid them on beds and couches, that at least the shadow of Peter might overshadow some of them." He said:

"Some centuries before our era the prophet, Isaiah, had a vision of the Messiah and exclaimed with rapture, 'Surely He bears our griefs and carries our sorrows.' And when the real Christ of Galilee afterward went about healing the sick the people said, 'He takes our infirmities and bears our sicknesses.'

"Thus it is the very essence of the Messianic spirit, so conceived in Bible times, for Christ to make all human sorrow His own sorrow and bear all our burdens as though they were His own. His Divine touch was expected to crowd poverty and sin and sorrow clear off the stage. Like an omnipotent magnet placed in the heart

of a perfect manhood, He is to fraternize all,
drawing them to His new creation as a kingdom of love.   This is the true Messianic kingdom, in which the wants of the weakest will
be supplied by the genius and power of the
strongest.

"The Messianic Healer is now in Denver.
His peculiar work is now showing to us one
great elemental force in the kingdom of God:
The element of a personal sacrifice in social
burden-bearing—after the teachings of Jesus.

"More than 15,000 people—mostly infirm—
have touched his hand.   Some have been
cured; very many have been helped, and thousands are saying, 'Surely he is a good man and
is doing good.'

"The common question to-day is, 'What do
you think of Schlatter?'   But in the face of
such facts as we are witnessing I am aware
that one man's opinion—least of all my own—
counts for little; it may become an offense to
truth.   And yet it is the clear duty of any religious teacher to inform himself concerning
this Healer and give the people whatever light
he thus obtains.   This is my apology for treating the subject to-night.

THE MAN.

"Francis Schlatter is a man in middle life, squarely built, strong in frame, Anglo-Saxon in complexion. He is medium in height, with long, dark hair parted in the middle. His face is large and honest, being brimful of candor and radiant with Christian trust. Like all famous shoemakers whose portraits have reached us, his facial expressions reveal less of wideness in thought, but more depth of faith. Looking upon the picture of Whittier, one may see why he pounded shoe pegs in getting his young soul ready to sing of Christ:

> "'Through all depths of sin and loss
> Drops the plummet of thy cross.'

"The Healer stands out of doors on the inside of the fence, grasping the hand and pressing in his left hand the handkerchief of each person in regular order who files past him on the walk outside.

"He is fittingly called 'the silent man,' and rarely speaks except to say as you pass from his grip, 'Thank you,' or 'Thank you, Jesus.' He works from 9 to 4, and wisely takes an hour at noon for lunch and rest. Near the hour for closing he leaves his stand, going into the street to mount a carriage and treat those who cannot enter the line because of weakness. No one in distress fails to attract his attention.

"He appears unconscious of what we call social distinctions. With a beneficence born of heaven and in the fullest imitation of Jesus, he has given up his life to relieve suffering humanity. He imposes no arbitrary conditions upon those who come for healing, but presumes that they have sufficient confidence in him to constitute what he calls Faith. And his profoundest joy appears to consist in the sacrifice of himself for the public good. He is getting thousands of letters from abroad and tries to answer a part of them. Handkerchiefs also come to him for his touch. He grants the request and returns them.

"With quick discernment he detects a bad case and bestows more time upon it. He never wants to know a disease. He will pause in his attention to the regular line and treat a very bad patient appealing to him from the outside crowd. In all this he shows such simple good sense that any sympathetic observer will be often stirred to deep emotion.

HAS COMMON FAITH-SENSE
ENLARGED?

"The economy of life in the universe has provided itself with three forces which extend
through all the range of human observation—
reason, Faith and sacrifice. They are original,
created by God, and in themselves are creative
of other forms of life, but not of life itself. The
higher grades of animals exhibit strength and
beauty with those instincts which approach
human reason. Children show remarkable
combinations of all three forces, with the sacri-
ficial element dominant—thus furnishing good
ground for the statement of Christ that a child
is a symbol of the kingdom of God. Education
will give dimension and grace to these func-
tions, but it cannot furnish them with power
nor supply their deficiency if the will declines
to exercise them.

THE GREATER QUESTION.

"Our first legitimate inquiry concerning this man is not whether he can cure the people of their physical ailments, or whether he wants to be known as a Messiah. Very possibly he may fail in many attempts at healing, and may at first entertain exaggerated notions of his own call from God. Yet he may not thereby fail to do much good, nor should we charge him with being a fanatic. Many a time in history has God illustrated Paul's rule of Providence in choosing weak things to confound the wise.

"But I am assured by those who worship with him at St. Patrick's church that he lays no claim to be the returning Christ, or the re-produced Messiah; that, on the contrary, his entire manner in private shows him to be conscious of himself only as a plain, guileless servant of Christ, taking his Master's word as exactly true and applicable to human needs in its own plainest terms. He refers everything to 'the Father,' and goes at his work with all the ardor of a perfect child of 'Father's will.'

"Our first question is, Does Francis Schlat-

ter bear the one test of original childlike obedience to God, as given us by the rule of Christ
for knowing who is in the kingdom of heaven?
Does he really show

> " 'Himself to nature's heart so near
> That all her voices in his ear'

Are the honest pulses of the Divine will,
urging him on to do good according to his ability and strength? And if he seem a little rash
or overknowing at first, he is quite likely to
come soon to the true consciousness of his mission, with greater wisdom and power. As Dr.
Arnot, of Scotland, once remarked to D. L.
Moody: 'The world has yet to see what a man
can do who is wholly consecrated to God.'

"He exhibits no trace of fanaticism, nor can
I find evidence that he has actually made any
extravagant self-assertion. I am assured that
he confesses that he does not understand all
the Bible, and humbly thinks himself called to
good works rather than teaching.

"His presence in the city has already proved
a benediction to a public audience. I never
saw so many people together in the street keep
so good order. He inspires a quiet reverence.
There is very little talk except when some one

who has been made whole comes in contact
with a rank disbeliever.

"The ultimate test of every Christian work
is in its power to subdue selfishness and in-
spire public faith in righteousness. Ethical
goodness, common sense, and both wrapped
within God's spirit, appear so far to be the
fruits by which Schlatter is to be known.
Should he continue with us and grow in his
good work, I venture to assert that he will in-
spire more true manhood than all our religious
teachings have yet accomplished. And the
managers of our coming carnival had better
begin to contemplate the event as a civic jubi-
lee.

HIS WORK.

"People will ask if he does actually cure.
We must first agree on what we mean by the
question. Comparatively few persons are absolutely cured from all liability to a germinal
return of a malignant disease. Medicine will
often help toward a cure by starting anew the
dormant forces of life. When medicine does
this, it may rather loosely be said to cure. It
does not actually do it. For all healing is ac-

complished only by nature, moving her po-
tencies along the avenues of vitality.

"Now, if Schlatter really starts these hidden energies, even though they do not continue
as long nor extend as far as we may wish, he
is thereby entitled to be called a Healer. But
he has produced effects which any physician
might call a cure. Rheumatism, sciatica, disease of the kidneys and Bright's disease are
cases brought to my notice by the subjects of
them who have received such signal results
from his treatment that only the word 'cured'
can tell the truth. Blindness has been slightly
relieved in many instances and very materially
helped in a few. Disordered vision has been
removed in at least one case of an engineer.
A barber whom I have—with other cases—
personally investigated, is at present, after
two weeks since treatment, as well as ever.
One is now preaching the gospel of healing
whose claim to a real cure will not be disputed.
I have received extraordinary benefit in the
case of a lameness of more than a year's standing. To my own mind nothing could be more
actual. It has been demonstrated that by a
ruse, a well man can be made to regard him-

self sick. And men have died under the false
impression that they were being killed. But
you could never convince the cases I have cited
that we have received no new life pulses from
the hand of Francis Schlatter.

"It is a gift altogether inestimable—even
though we had less physical good to report—
when one is sent to stand up in such Divine
manhood and throw over the city such a Messianic shadow.

INCIDENTS.

"One can hear considerable Bible language
revived at the healing. Things get to glowing
once in a while. Some one in the crowd produced a scrap from one of Myron Reed's sermons, and was ready to stand by the issue and
defend the quotation against the world, the
flesh and the devil. The passage was in Acts,
xix. But another man sawed the atmosphere
to convince us that the book of Acts runs out
before it comes to the nineteenth chapter. I
noticed that a number of decent-looking people vowed if ever they got home again they
would read the old mother's Bible once more,

so as to converse intelligently upon the me-
chanical arrangement of Acts.

"Two sharp-eyed ladies approached a group
of people and produced their handkerchiefs to
show what the clairvoyant did. 'Oh,' said
number 3, 'then it is like Christian Science, is
it?' 'Yes, like mind cure you say.' I retired
from the scene with a small slice of a London
fog in my mentality.

"If any man can witness the simple trust of
the crowds of people that gather there; if he
can stand in the throng and note the approach
of some carriage, wherein a liveried coachman
brings a pale sufferer to this fountain of hope;
or if he can watch the poor, weak woman on
her crutches and the emaciated sons of toil,
outworn in the fierce struggle for existence—
all forgetting that they have any social distinctions, as they act out life's real drama—if
day after day he can witness this without his
heart breaking into tears, he can do more than
I am able to do.

WILL THIS HEALING EFFECT ENDURE?

"Probably not longer than conditions endure which promote it. We dare not assume that the miracles of Jesus produced longevity, or that they gave more than temporary relief. Lazarus certainly died after having been raised from the dead. The point is not very material. But the home story of Mary and Martha, made grateful by the presence of Jesus, and affording Him opportunity to do the vastly more important work of teaching the gospel, becomes a source of Faith to mankind, even though their brother had died the next week.

"We are not sure that the acorns from the hand of Paul, or the shadow of Peter, covered a lengthy period of health to any one. We can only know that these apostles of the Master gave to the people of that day a little comfort and took from them some burdens and sorrows of life. They were the Messianic shadow of their Lord, the Great Healer.

"An eminent author of our day, writing on social economy, says: 'All that keeps the earth from being heaven is the self-will of man,

which refuses to know and do the will of God.'
And in his vision of Sir Launfal searching for
the holy grail, Lowell sings:

> " 'Not only around our infancy
> Doth heaven with all its splendors lie;
> Daily, with souls that cringe and plot,
> We Sianais climb and know it not.'

" 'For a cap and bells our lives we pay,
　Baubles we buy with a whole soul's tasking;
'Tis heaven alone that is given away,
　'Tis only God may be had for the asking.'

SOURCE OF HIS POWER.

" 'Magnetism,' says one. 'Yes, he's full of
it,' echoes a good second. Grant the claim.
What, then, is magnetism—an interpretation
of the devil, or is it one of our Creator's chosen
agencies for healing and conserving life? The
latter, most certainly. Christ was so charged
with magnetism—or some other power Divine
and exactly equivalent—that His garments
were full of it. Some years ago, when Professor
Winchell published 'Sketches of Creation,' I
asked him upon what grounds geologists find
man so remote in the history of the rocks. He

replied that he did not accept the hypothesis, but preferred to bring antiquity nearer to the recent age of man. Allow me to use this form of words to declare my conviction that nature brings God infinitely near to man, instead of shoving itself, like a series of mill screens, be-tween Him and His noblest work in man. Em-erson puts it uniquely but correctly in saying that the relation between mind and matter stands in the will of God, and calls the world an 'incarnation of God.' And in the accurate perception of the Bible, that God is known by His works, I am sure the sage of Concord is right. George Herbert declares that

" 'More servants will wait on man
Than he'll take notice of. In every path
He treads down that which doth befriend him
When sickness makes him pale and wan.'

"The French savant, M. Guizot, used to re-mark that if we accept the general proposition that 'God is,' all else becomes easy and natural. Then we all say, 'Let the magnetic link, the Faith link, the social link, or anything God has made useful, be employed to work human sal-vation and joy.' For they are all of God, and will not meet in opposition. 'Imagination'

explains it to some who take a superficial view
of the phenomena. Very well. The Creator
has certainly provided much important work
for this faculty of imagining things. One day
in the early half of our century a few gentlemen sat conversing in the cabin of a North Atlantic steamer, bound for Europe. A Catholic
priest was present and told how he had just
imagined a submarine cable for sending mes-
sages across the ocean. It was a mere 'imagination,' you know, but God put it into the
heart of Cyrus Field to build thereby one un-
broken line between the nations. Columbus
imagined a continent beyond the setting sun
of Italian skies, and by the aid of Spain found
that God had actually placed that land on his
map some centuries before the Santa Maria
sailed. And here we all repeat, if you will,
'Yes, imagination has a good part to play in
this drama of life. God bless imagination and
give us more of it.'

"Yet it is a very feeble way of telling the
truth about these phenomena of Schlatter.
Let us be frank with our Father and call it the
work of God; for not until the heavenly Father
sends some one, Field, Columbus or the Healer,
will the components combine to produce the
12

result. I say it with no thought of lowering his grade, that I believe Brother Schlatter is a heaven-sent servant to perform a specific work among us. And for any man or woman to openly and knowingly oppose him is blasphemous; to do it ignorantly is more than foolish.

"I find that some of Mr. Schlatter's patients get healing without faith, some begin with curiosity and reach the point of confidence before touching his hand. One man feels the genuine battery shock; a dozen others feel nothing of the kind. One woman from New Mexico told me she felt so weak under the wrenchings of some power that twisted her, she thought she would die.

"One fellow came walking briskly back again down the line, stopping often to tell the crowds about him; that 'Schlatter spells his name with two t's; he's a Catholic and I'm an A. P. A., but I don't care a nickel who heals me!'

"Much that we call Faith, in the Bible is meant to imply only simple obedience. The churches have imposed an artificial meaning on this grace of Faith. A rational surrender to eternal goodness, in a spirit of obedience to righteousness, is the heart of faith. If the clergy would teach the truth in its native simplicity it wouldn't be long before all would come to a reasonable exercise of Faith.

INSTANTANEOUS EFFECT.

"Some will demand instantaneous effect. But it is not needed in this age of scientific growth. To set in motion the hiding pulses of vitality is just as good a work to-day as to have put the impotent man on his feet in the first century. Even Christ took time. In one case a blind man at first saw only trees walking as men.

"We do wrong to judge Schlatter's work by the material standard of the first Messianic miracles.

"Is surgery impossible by any one except an expert? Is the North Pole the only magnet because it is the greatest? Our silent brother across the Platte may not be an expert yet. He may grow vastly. He will if he preserves his obedient humility. The meek shall inherit the earth. Even now he throws a greater Messianic shadow over our city than all others combined.

"Not all will be healed in body. It is the
mission of some to suffer for the world's healing. Chloe Lankton was a shoemaker's daughter in New England. For forty years she lay
on her bed of pain, so sweetened by the sacri-
ficial element that her life became a gospel to
multitudes. Literature has been made sacri-
ficial by such sufferers as Robert Louis Steven-
son, Parkman and Milton. It is this kind of literature that is so rapidly winning the earth
and expelling that heathenish distinction between the sacred and the secular. Christ laid
more stress on the act of giving a cup of cold
water to a thirsty sufferer on the desert of life
than upon all his miracles. For what else are
we millions related to each other, but to become Messianic? We may drink and feel better, we may thirst again, but the true Messianic spirit of healing, once becoming common
after the order of Jesus and Schlatter, and a
few such dissolving views of humanity will
soon make our earth a heaven.

"This old prophetic idea became a longing
of man, and Christ wove it into the seamless
robe of His life. Dr. Franklin said: 'Whoever
introduces into public affairs the principles of
primitive Christianity will change the face of

the world.' Let society also assume a Messianic spirit and see that henceforth no idle hand
need fail to earn an honest living, and no cry
of want return to a fraternized earth.

"Let our clergymen and our churches begin
to cast this Divine shadow. Brothers, this is
our opportunity. Let us pray the Father to
give greater power to Brother Schlatter. I
suggest that you make a specialty of asking
God to embue him with the power of Christ.
It would be the most wonderful prayer-meet-
ing ever held in Denver. Let Trinity church
be opened to him, that he may have comfort to
impart to the crowds that throng him on these
frosty mornings. This is your day to save the
people and society by the soothing Messianic
Shadow."

FRANCIS SCHLATTER.

A pure bright star aflame with love
Divine, yes holy, 'twas so pure and chaste
Simply obeying the Father's will.
Commanding our troubles and diseases "be stil ;"
Trying ever unto us to show
The love that is centred on us here below;
Believing the word which he daily read,
If ye have but the faith of a mustard seed,
Great miracles you shall perform indeed.
You shall cast out diseases and raise the dead,
And cause the sea to forsake its bed,
And the mountains to crumble to dust.

Standing apart, yet amongst the city's roar,
Thou stoodst with bared head and eyes upturned
As they stood before him in one long array.
The poor, the rich, the sad, the gay,
The crippled, the blind, and those sorely distressed
Turned from Thee happy for they were blessed.

We trace the Healer after leaving Elizabeth, Colorado, in a southerly direction, always keeping very close to the Union Pacific, Denver & Gulf railroad tracks. At a point directly south of Elizabeth we found him at a place called Walsenburg, which is a small place, but very important on account of its vast coal mines. This place did not detain him long, as he was soon after discovered at Rouse, Colorado. This was on the 27th of November, a little over two weeks after leaving Denver. The Healer was still riding his white horse, and as he rode into town with his white slouch hat and dark suit, together with his long hair, which was under his hat and confined by a woolen turban, he was not easily recognized at first appearance. Behind his saddle were rolled his blankets, and over his shoulder was swung a large canteen, which held at least a gallon of water. He was asked if he would not stop, to which the Healer replied he had not time. In a very short time the streets were filled with people and children, and he was followed by a large crowd who had gathered about him, but to all he said he could not stop, and he did not, but went on his way. It was indeed a queer crowd that escorted, or rather followed, him out of town, some mounted on bicycles, some on saddle horses, some in buggies. Above the town of Walsenburg is a large hill, and it was at this point that the Healer stopped and shook hands with all who came to him. Many of the crowd went back to the town, but a large number followed the Healer into Rouse.

When it became known that the Healer had passed through Rouse and was on his way south, scores of people set out after him to overtake him and shake hands with him. The Healer refused none, and carefully held the hands of all for a few minutes. When asked where he was going he invariably replied, "I do not know. The Father is directing me, and I expect to go where I will be alone and can commune with the Father undisturbed. My powers are increasing every day, but the Father tells me I must have rest, and so I go. I left Denver because my time was up. I did not intend to stay any longer. The large number of railroad men who came from the East to see me and found me gone will be benefited just as much as if they had seen me. I do not do the healing; it is the Father; and to be healed all must have Faith. My future I know nothing about; but if it is His will, my mission will be carried on as it has been in the past."

The Healer carried nothing to eat, and he only wanted something to eat once a day, and that was given to him by the people who lived along the road. He drank large quantities of water, which accounted for the large canteen which he carried across his shoulder.

At the residence of W. C. Johnson he treated a child. It was an affecting sight to see the great, strong man, with hands like those of a giant. The Healer took the small hand of the child into his, which he held for twenty minutes. Every now and then he drew upon the whole strength of his body, and it seemed as though he was lifting a great load and every muscle in his body was strained. The child looked at him confidingly and laid its head on his hand. The scene at the house where the Healer made his short stay while at Rouse was certainly a remarkable one. Some women stood tearfully by with Faith as perfectly visioned as it was of old. The mothers kissed their babes, just blessed, if only for their hope. And so the silent man came and left, and in a few, very few, minutes of his calling he left in some homes many thankful hearts for the coming. There were tears of thankfulness in some eyes and hopes of betterment and joy in some faces that, ere long, the weary, sore and disabled bodies would take on a new dress of health and strength. A colored lady was treated and went away with the tears streaming down her cheeks. Nothing induced him to remain in Rouse, and although a warm supper was provided for him, he refused to partake of it. His horse, however, was well fed.

The movements of the Healer were recorded after leaving Rouse as having passed through Santa Clara, Colorado. From Acquillar, a small town in the great coal region of Southern Colorado, the Healer was traced to Hastings, another large mining camp. The streets were lined with people, who anxiously awaited the arrival of Schlatter in Trinidad, but the people were doomed to disappointment, the Healer having pursued his southerly course.

After leaving Colorado Francis entered New Mexico, from whence he left some months before. The Healer was soon lost track of when he went among the Mexicans and Indians, miles from any railroad or village.

Nothing further was learned of his movements or whereabouts until the following year, and it was during the month of February that the Healer was located on a ranch at Datil, New Mexico, where he was resting. Towards the latter part of the month of May of this year, word was received from Ada Morley Jarrett, who lives at Hermosillo Ranch, New Mexico, at whose place Francis was staying. In her letter she stated that the Healer thinks he may be in Colorado again, but at present he is on his way to Old Mexico, healing the sick and spreading happiness as he goes along. In substance the letter from Hermosillo Ranch ran as follows: "You ask for a letter on Schlatter, and your kindly insistance reminds me of certain stories Mr. Schlatter told me of experiences in the Fox residence, in Denver. 'Often people were refused,' said he, 'the first time, for the Father wanted me to just try their Faith, but if they came a second or third time, well, Father said, "Let them come in."'

"I appreciate that the knowledge I have is of such transcendant value and beauty that to share it with others would be a blessing to both; nevertheless the What and the When is an ironclad trust, and impossible for me to violate. The Where, however, he gave me latitude in, and told me to manage it to suit myself, which in the near future I shall try to do. I realize the value of his long, long rest here, but he often said, 'Father told me in Colorado, when I asked for rest, "You will have a long rest in Southwestern New Mexico." I said to Father, "Well, it will have to be a very quiet, peculiar ranch where I can have rest." "It is," He told me.'

"It is not yet the exact time or place, When and Where he gave me permission to talk, and I can say only a little. He often, in that Divinely gentle method and manner, would say: 'Father is good to me,' and I added 'Yes,' for once remembering all too vividly his eloquent detailed description of how he suffered on that horrible tramp of two years in hunger and cold, poverty and humiliation, and again I hear the gentle tones, 'Father is very good to let me stay so long. I did not think it when I came. It is the first real rest and peace I have had since mother died.' Schlatter's manner could be severe as well as gentle, and when I showed him that 'Globe-Democrat' dispatch from Socorro, were he on the material plane I should say he seemed disgusted. Said he: 'Now just look at that; your ranch isn't 150 miles from Socorro. I've not spoken to a soul save the two trusty friends, and Father says they won't talk. No one has ever seen me, yet they telegraph those stories over the land. And fast! I wonder what they think? Do they think Father wants me to suffer forever? Do they think it is an easy thing to go forty days and forty nights without food? Ah, it's no easy thing! I told Father, "You must give the spiritual food or I perish." I don't think Father will ever require that of me again. I hope not, for disobedience is not in me. But one such fast ought to set people thinking. That is all Father wants. He wants His children on the earth to-day to think—think.'

"Schlatter would pace the floor and stride across the canon with such a determined air, I often laughed to myself and did not wonder they called him the 'Cyclone' in the Hot Springs jail in 1893, when the voice said, 'Follow me'—that Inaudible, Invisible, Invincible Power he hears, heeds, and in which he lives, moves and has his being—took him as a tramp to prospect for souls on that awful walk across this continent, in poverty, hunger and dirt, and landed him in jail to study justice and men's methods, among other pathetic experiences in the bygone years.

"Of course his prolonged stay here was a surprise to those who knew, but he is of such marvelous make-up, his life is so beyond criticism, his whole mission to help humanity, that the people have a right to know all he is willing they should know. But I am the one he told to keep still. It is easy to see my position and my duty. It is a sacred trust, one I know is of responsibility, and in which I shall take good care not to blunder."

Francis continued to live on this ranch until the latter part of March, when he again started to heal amongst the Indians and Mexicans of New Mexico. From the best information we can obtain, he is still there.

THE END.